Tears welled in Riya's eyes.

It was ridiculous how susceptible she was to Dhruv, and how easily he could hurt her even without trying. He'd probably be bewildered if he knew that she was upset at the thought of him meeting a lineup of prospective brides, and she couldn't blame him. He'd made no promises to her, no commitments—only asked for some time together to get to know each other. A request that she was now almost a hundred percent sure she should have refused. So much for trying to act like a sophisticated woman of the world. She was still the stupid lovesick girl she'd been in college, and the quicker she accepted it the better.

This is Shoma Narayanan's fabulous first book!

We couldn't be more excited about this uniquely talented author.

Her witty, contemporary writing will take you to a whole new world of romance!

Keep a look out for more titles by Shoma, coming soon....

SHOMA NARAYANAN

Monsoon Wedding Fever

HARLEQUIN®
entertain, enrich, inspire™

Recycling programs
for this product may
not exist in your area.

ISBN-13: 978-0-373-17844-5

MONSOON WEDDING FEVER

First North American Publication 2012

Shoma Narayanan started reading Harlequin® Romance novels at the age of eleven, borrowing them from neighbors and hiding them inside textbooks so that her parents didn't find out. At that time the thought of writing one herself never entered her head—she was convinced she wanted to be a teacher when she grew up. When she was a little older she decided to become an engineer instead, and took a degree in electronics and telecommunications. Then she thought a career in management was probably a better bet, and went off to do an MBA. That was a decision she never regretted, because she met the man of her dreams in the first year of B-school; fifteen years later they're married with two adorable kids, whom they're raising with the same careful attention to detail that they gave their second-year project on organizational behavior.

A couple of years ago Shoma took up writing as a hobby (after successively trying her hand at baking, sewing, knitting, crochet and patchwork), and was amazed at how much she enjoyed it. Now she works grimly at her banking job through the week, and tries to balance writing with household chores during weekends. Her family has been unfailingly supportive of her latest hobby, and are also secretly very, very relieved that they don't have to eat, wear or display the results.

This is Shoma's first book!

To my mom, who believed in romance,
and to my dad, who didn't.

CHAPTER ONE

'*DUBEYJI, UTHO*. Wake up!' Riya hissed at the watchman snoring away behind the locked gates of her apartment building.

It was a Friday, and she'd gone out for dinner with a bunch of colleagues in central Mumbai to celebrate a deal they'd just cracked. She'd not bothered to check if the gate was open when her friends dropped her off, and now she was standing all alone on a deserted and not very safe road in the middle of the night, dressed in form-fitting black and fake designer jewellery. She pulled her scarf around her a little more closely as a pair of young men roared past her on a bike. For a minute she contemplated calling her flatmate—only he had a cousin coming down from Singapore that evening, and was likely to be out partying as well.

The snoring rose to a crescendo as Dubeyji settled himself into a more comfortable spot on his plastic chair. Riya rattled the gate a few times, then picked up a handful of little blue pebbles from one of the fancy flowerpots flanking the entrance. The third pebble did the trick, shaking Dubeyji out of what was probably a most interesting dream starring a bevy of luscious Bhojpuri beauties.

'*Yeh koi time hai, ghar aane ka*—madam, is this

any time to come home?' he grumbled as he unlocked the gate.

Dubeyji hadn't got over his disapproval yet that the multinational firm Riya worked for provided accommodation for both male *and* female employees. He still liked Riya, though, partly because she looked a bit like his favourite movie star, and partly because she came from his part of the country.

Riya was still giggling to herself when she reached the flat, remembering Dubeyji's outraged expression when the pebble hit him. It took her a minute to open the door—Gaurav had dutifully left it on the latch. He had, however, neglected to leave a single light on, and the living room was in complete and utter darkness when she finally got in.

'Dumb idiot,' she said out loud, and then she struggled to get her strappy high-heeled sandals off in the dark. 'Damn these shoes!'

Barefoot at last, she began padding across the room—to find herself suddenly tripping and falling down in a heap right onto the warm, hard, very muscular and very male body sprawled across the middle of the floor.

For a wild moment Riya wondered if she was in the wrong flat. Then, as she yelped in alarm and tried to push herself off the man, an amused voice drawled in her ear.

'Gaurav's missing flatmate, I presume?'

By then she'd found her footing, and she bounced off in a hurry and snapped a switch on. Bright fluorescent light bathed the room as she glared at the man trying to get free of the scarf that had landed on his face. An extremely appealing-looking man, she thought, her annoyance abating as she took in the perfectly sculpted physique, the rumpled hair, and...hang on...the extremely familiar face. Not to mention the extremely, familiar golden-brown eyes, blinking now as they adjusted to the bright light, and the *excruciatingly* familiar, eminently kissable lips, and the strong hands, with their long, sensitive fingers...

'Dhruv Malhotra!' she wailed, sitting down abruptly on the nearest sofa.

'Shh...people are sleeping inside,' he said, his deep voice with its slight gravelly undertone as sexy as ever.

'But—but I don't understand,' Riya stammered. 'What are you doing here? Are *you* Gaurav's cousin?'

Dhruv nodded, standing up from the makeshift bed spread out on the floor.

Riya automatically ran her eyes over him. Even in a ratty black vest and faded jogging bottoms, he looked gorgeous. He'd filled out since college—the once boyish frame had morphed into a body worthy of an athlete, all lean limbs, broad shoulders and taut muscle.

'I'm sorry I couldn't warn you—I figured out you lived here only when we arrived and I saw your name on the door. We came in quite late and I thought we could deal with the situation in the morning—I wasn't expecting you to fall over me.'

'And you were sleeping right in the middle of the living room because...?'

'My kid sister decided to come along at the last moment, so she's in the spare room and there was no place left for me.' He flashed her a sudden grin. 'I didn't think you'd appreciate coming home and finding me in your bed.'

'You're right. I wouldn't have,' Riya said firmly.

She walked up to him and took the scarf from him, willing herself not to touch his hand while she did so.

She'd thought about him a lot in the twelve years since they'd last met, and rehearsed countless scenarios in which she confronted him/pretended he didn't exist/made crazy, wild love to him... Now that they were finally face to face, all she wanted to do was run away and keep going.

'Goodnight, Dhruv.'

'Riya?'

She turned. He was looking at her, an oddly appealing glimmer in his eyes.

'It's good to see you again.'

Riya gave him a tight little smile and went on to her room without answering.

Dhruv switched off the light and got back into bed. He'd been awake when Riya came in, and had smiled to himself when he'd heard her cursing in her adorably husky voice. Seeing her again had been more of a jolt than he'd expected, even though he had been mentally prepared. She had changed. Not so much in appearance, though she'd probably put on a few kilos—she'd been waif-like in college, so thin that he'd been able to pick her up with one hand, but so energetic and full of life that she'd seemed twice her real size. Now she'd developed some womanly curves—as he'd discovered when she landed on top of him.

For a few seconds he'd been tempted to drag her closer, enjoy the feeling of her soft breasts heavy on his arm and her silky hair spread over his chest. Her hair had been short in college, and she'd always been bundled either into a shapeless *salwar kameez*—the traditional Asian tunic and loose trousers—or an oversized T-shirt and scruffy jeans. She looked far more sophisticated now, with figure-hugging clothes and long, wavy perfectly styled hair cascading down her back.

Her face was unchanged, with large eyes, sooty eye-lashes, flawless dusky skin, rosebud mouth and dainty little tip-tilted nose all present and correct. The eyes were wary, though. Nowhere near as open or as trust-ing as they'd used to be.

Dhruv punched his pillow in frustration. Five min-utes and the woman had already got him tied up in knots. He should make some excuse to Gaurav and move into a hotel for the remaining two days he needed to be in Mumbai. On the other hand Gaurav was get-ting married in a week, and the whole point of this visit was to spend time with him before the wedding—they'd been very close when they were younger, but hadn't met in the last six years. Moving out wasn't the best option—perhaps he should try talking to Riya, laying old ghosts to rest.

Riya latched the door to her room and slowly started clearing the mess of books off her bed. Dhruv still af-fected her strongly, she noted, feeling extremely dis-pleased with herself.

Over the years she'd come to believe that he had only managed to completely bowl her off her feet because he'd been the first really attractive man she'd come across in the seventeen years she'd spent growing up in a small, conservative North Indian university town. Her schoolmates had been OK, but she'd known them all her life, and the fact that some were male hadn't re-ally registered even when she was in her teens. It was difficult to lust after someone you'd seen peeing in their pants in kindergarten!

In college Dhruv had stood out among a largely nerdy and uncouth crowd like…like a peacock in a yard full of sparrows. Or, she thought, trying to think of a more appropriate simile, a Swiss chocolate in a bowl of peppermints. Or a Ferrari in a line-up of taxis.

But after college she'd met at least a dozen men who displayed at least as good a combination of looks and brains as Dhruv, and not a single one of them had made her heart race the teensiest bit. Not Sandeep, the hottest man on her graduate course, nor Sikandar, serial heartbreaker and her second boss. Not Marcelo, the drop-dead gorgeous Brazilian she'd met in a training course last year. Not Vinay, whom she'd dated for almost two years before deciding not to marry him. Not even Anurag, the CFO of one of her top corporate clients. Well, maybe Anurag. Just a little bit. Even though he was married and at least fifteen years older than her. But compared to the effect Dhruv had on her even Anurag faded into insignificance.

'Concentrate on the bad things,' Riya told herself firmly, chewing on her toothbrush fiercely. 'He walked away from you without any explanation whatsoever—' she spat into the sink and rinsed her mouth vigorously '—and never bothered to get in touch with you afterwards.'

She climbed into her pyjamas and got into bed. She lay for a while looking up at the ceiling, remembering the feeling of utter bewilderment and loss that had stayed with her every waking minute for months after Dhruv had stepped out of her life. Even now just thinking about it made her feel empty inside… Humiliating as it was to admit, unless she was very, very careful she was in just as much danger of falling for him now as she had been when she was seventeen.

'Pathetic, man-crazy moron,' she said sternly to herself, but it didn't help. Not when Dhruv lay stretched out on the floor in the next room. So close…

'*He might be married,*' the pragmatic part of her brain prompted, and her eyes flew open at the thought. No, he wasn't married—she distinctly remembered Gaurav saying that his cousin was single, thank goodness. Not that it should affect her; she shouldn't care even if he'd turned Mormon and married seven wives.

Riya finally managed to fall asleep around five a.m., and slept soundly till well after nine. She was still groggy when Ranjana, their stickler of a cook-cleaner, marched firmly into her room and prodded her awake.

'*Utho, didi*—wake up. Everyone else woke up hours ago.'

'Good for them,' Riya mumbled, rolling over in bed.

'The little *didi* also just woke up.'

Riya opened her eyes, wondering if Dhruv had been enterprising enough to smuggle a girlfriend into the flat. Or not. Hadn't he said his sister had come down with him? Curiosity stirred. Dhruv had talked a lot about his kid sister when they were in college. She must be around twenty now, as she was some twelve years younger than him. Clearly an afterthought on the part of their parents, but her older brother adored her.

Dhruv was sitting at the breakfast table watching Gaurav efficiently work his way through a triple-egg omelette and a small mountain of buttered toast. If possible, Dhruv looked even better than he had the previous night. His hair was damp from the shower and curling slightly at the nape of his neck, and his white T-shirt set off the honey-gold of his skin perfectly. Riya's treacherous heart started doing a little jig of excitement inside her chest. Evidently the previous night's self-administered homily had gone to waste.

'Hey there, Sleeping Beauty!' Gaurav said as he caught sight of Riya. 'Come here—meet my cousin.'

Dhruv gave her a brief smile that didn't quite reach his eyes.

'We've met,' Riya said, sliding into the chair opposite her stocky flatmate. 'Gaurav, *don't* use the jam knife for the butter—no wonder the chicken butter masala Ranjana made last week was pink!'

'I thought that was for Valentine's Day,' Gaurav said cheerfully. 'I've suspected Ranjana of nursing a secret passion for me for the last five years.'

'Who's Ranjana—the cook?' A curvy, impish-looking girl walked into the room. She was wearing a black T-shirt with a skull embroidered on it—the skull sported a pink bow—and the matching pyjama trousers had 'Sweet Devil' embroidered over the butt in pink.

'Look who's awake!' Gaurav said. 'Riya, this is Chutki—Dhruv's little sister and officially the most painful brat alive. Chutki, say hello to Riya like a good girl.'

Chutki stuck her tongue out at him. 'Stop calling me by my nickname. It makes me sound like a two-year-old. Hi, I'm Drishti,' she said, smiling at Riya. Then she looked a little closer. 'Hey, you look awfully familiar. Have we met?'

'I don't think so,' Riya replied, wondering if Dhruv had told his sister something about her.

She'd never met Chutki before, but she'd heard a lot about his cute little sister. She was the only person in Dhruv's family that he'd ever talked about. They had a brother, too, who was a couple of years younger than Dhruv, she remembered, but Dhruv had only mentioned him once in passing, saying that he was crazy about photography. He'd never talked about his parents, giving evasive answers to even the most pointed questions, and very early on in their relationship Riya had learnt not to ask too many questions about them.

Chutki was still observing Riya closely, trying to puzzle something out.

'I get it,' she said suddenly. 'Dhruv—doesn't she look just like that girl whose photo you used to keep hidden in your cupboard?'

Riya couldn't help it. Her cheeks flamed in embarrassment and Gaurav, who'd opened his mouth to make a wisecrack, shut it hastily after one look at her face.

Dhruv looked up.

'Thanks, Chutki.' He'd been furious with her when she'd found a faded photograph of Riya hidden under a stack of T-shirts in his cupboard, and he'd caught her and shaken her hard when she'd gone dancing out of his room with the photo to show it to their mother. He still remembered the shock on her little face, the tears filling her eyes—it was the first time her beloved big brother had lost his temper with her.

She looked almost as upset now. 'You mean she's the same... Oh, God, I'm so sorry. Open mouth, change feet—that's me. But if you guys know each other, how come you didn't realise you were...?' She shut up abruptly as Dhruv gave her a look.

'It was a long time ago—we knew each other in college,' said Dhruv curtly, wishing he'd never been a sentimental idiot and hung on to the photograph. 'We haven't been in touch since then.'

'Oh, right,' Gaurav said easily. 'I knew you went to the same college. Never thought to ask Riya if she knew you. I just assumed you'd have graduated before she joined. Given how ancient you are and all.'

Dhruv smiled. 'I'm three years older than the two of you. Architecture is a five-year course, remember?'

He was hoping that they were safely off the topic—he could see that Riya had tensed up, and it boded ill for his chances of having any kind of sensible conversation on the subject with her later on. He hadn't reckoned on his little sister's never-ending curiosity, though.

'You were dating, weren't you? Why'd you split up?' Chutki asked, interested.

Suddenly Riya had had enough. 'We weren't dating,' she said crisply. 'We were friends and, like Dhruv said, he was three years ahead of me. We didn't stay in touch after he left college.'

Chutki looked a little abashed, and Riya felt guilty about snapping at her. It wasn't her fault. She was just curious, and she belonged to the reality TV generation in which everyone discussed their past and current relationships in loud and public detail. She'd probably be hugely amused if she knew how Riya went all shivery and tingly each time she looked at Dhruv.

Riya pushed her chair back from the table. 'I'm done,' she said. 'I'm going down to the gym for an hour. You guys staying in? Or do you plan to go out?'

Gaurav said, 'We haven't decided yet. Dhruv wants to buy something for Madhulika, only I'm not sure what she'd like. I was hoping you'd have some ideas…'

'Given that you're marrying the woman in a week, I'd have expected *you* to have some clue,' Riya retorted, irritated at her flatmate for trying to palm off the decision onto her. 'If you can't think of something yourself, try Googling "gift ideas for morons".'

'I'll make her come up with something,' Gaurav said to Dhruv as he got up to clear the dishes. 'She's spent hours chatting to Madhulika on the phone about the wedding. By the way, I've never seen her being this snippy, and I've known her for some years now. Bad break-up?'

Dhruv shook his head, irritated with his cousin. 'We weren't in a relationship. I told you. *She* told you. What does it take to drive that simple fact into your skull?'

'A lot more than just you idiots telling me so every two minutes,' Gaurav said tartly. 'You may not have been dating, but you were definitely not "just good friends". Sparks fly all over the place when you look at each other.'

He would have probably continued in that vein for a few more minutes if Riya's door hadn't opened. She came out wearing a no-nonsense sleeveless navy vest with a pair of dry-fit tracksuit bottoms. The outfit had obviously been chosen for comfort rather than elegance, but the stretchy material of the top clung to her near-perfect hourglass figure in a way that made Dhruv's mouth immediately go dry.

She hardly looked at him on her way out, just pausing to say over her shoulder, 'Order the groceries, please, Gaurav. Ranjana's made a list.'

'Just good friends,' Gaurav muttered, taking in Dhruv's expression as he continued gazing at the door a good five minutes after Riya had shut it behind her.

Dhruv stood up abruptly. 'I have some work calls to make,' he said. 'And, if we're going out, isn't it about time you had a wash and changed? Unless, of course, you're planning to stun Mumbai with a glimpse of those psychedelic pyjamas.'

Gaurav grimaced and went to the bathroom. Dhruv was still his favourite cousin, but his tongue was as barbed as ever—he made a mental note not to bug him about Riya ever again.

* * *

'For God's sake, Chang, you should be able to handle this!' Dhruv exploded forty minutes later.

He strode over to the window and looked out, frowning as his second-in-command launched into a lengthy explanation for the current crisis at work. He very rarely lost his temper with his team, but he was now at the end of his tether. This trip wasn't going as planned, he thought as he closed the call, cutting off his employee's explanation midway. He'd been unnecessarily harsh with Chang, and he knew the reason had nothing to do with work. Meeting Riya had unsettled him more than he would have imagined possible.

He'd thought of her often since they'd parted—for many years the memory of how he'd treated her had filled him with guilt, and an unexplained feeling of anger. She'd been head-over-heels in love with him, and he'd spurned her without much of an explanation. At that time he had thought he was acting for the best, but in hindsight he'd acted like an immature idiot.

He'd known very early on that they didn't have a future together. For a twenty-year-old, he'd had very fixed ideas, utterly convinced by his parents' disastrous marriage that falling in love was a mug's game. Till he met Riya, he'd never even been tempted. She'd been doing an undergraduate degree in Computer Science, while he'd been in his final year of his architecture course, and the first time he'd met her what had struck him was her vitality—her enthusiasm for life. It had stepped out of her and grabbed him around the throat before he'd known what was happening. She was beautiful as well, and intelligent, but those were things that he'd noticed only later.

Dhruv grimly thought back to how he'd deluded himself for several months, trying to think of her as an

interesting companion—more of an intellectual spar-
ring partner than a flesh-and-blood woman. Reality
had hit while he'd been helping her with an engineering drawing assignment, leaning over her shoulder to
loosen her death-grip on the pencil. Her hair had smelt
of lemons and tangerines, and as she'd turned laugh-
ingly towards him he'd looked into her wide cinnamon
eyes and found himself unable to look away. The sudden attraction had blindsided him, shaking him temporarily out of the carefully erected emotional barriers
he had surrounded himself with.

She'd stopped mid-sentence when she'd seen the
naked longing in his eyes, and blushed deeply, her long,
sooty eyelashes dropping down to cover her eyes. If
nothing else, Dhruv thought wryly, that was the only
time he'd ever seen her at a loss for words. Nothing had
been said, but there had been a new kind of awareness
between them from that day onwards, an always present undercurrent of sexual tension that had made the
simplest gestures take on immense significance.

A door slammed in the flat, and Dhruv's thoughts
jerked back to the present. Riya was home. She was
sweating slightly after her hour in the gym, and her
cheeks were slightly flushed. Dhruv felt his heartbeat
accelerate as he saw her—his first thought was that this
was exactly how she'd look after being made love to,
and he shook himself mentally to get rid of the further
images that this conjured up. A second wave of lust hit
him as he noticed the hint of cleavage that showed as
she bent down to untie the laces of her gym shoes, and
he looked hastily away.

Riya checked for a second when she saw Dhruv in
the living room. She'd been half hoping that he'd be
out of the house by the time she returned, so that she

wouldn't have to struggle to keep up the coolly sophisticated front she'd donned. Her initial impulse was to run to her room, but she forced herself to walk slowly—partly because she didn't want Dhruv to think he affected her in any way, and partly because she didn't want to trip and fall flat on her face. Her sense of balance had improved significantly since college days, when she'd fallen over at least once a week, but she didn't trust herself while Dhruv was around.

'Where's Gaurav?' she heard herself ask.

'Gone for a bath. By the way, he's still not come up with any ideas for a gift for Madhulika, so if you can think of something I'd be really, really grateful.'

He smiled up at her, and Riya found herself unable to tear her eyes away from him. He was still impossibly good-looking, she decided. A beam of sunlight from the window glinted off his dark brown hair and highlighted the honey-gold planes of his almost perfectly chiselled face. His lips were just the right shape—not too thin, and not too full—quirking up a little at the corners to offset the firm cast of his jaw. But his best features were still his eyes—golden-brown with flecks of green, framed in impossibly long lashes.

Something in his expression finally cued her that she'd been staring at him like an idiot.

'Gift?' she repeated, parrot-like, dragging her eyes away from his. 'A watch, maybe?'

Dhruv was still looking at her and she kept talking, as if the sound of her own voice would keep her from doing something moderately embarrassing, like reaching a hand out to brush back the straight hair falling over his forehead, or really, really stupid, like flinging herself into his arms.

'Madhu collects watches, and there's a new one with

a purple dial she likes—Gaurav won't get it for her because he has this crazy theory about watches being a countdown till the day you die.'

'Yes, I know about that one,' Dhruv said drily. 'It also explains why he's late for pretty much everything. Thanks for the idea, Riya.'

Riya said politely that he was most welcome, and escaped to her room to collapse onto the bed and stare at the ceiling. Dhruv had changed, she thought. She'd known him very well at one time, and she could sense that something fundamental about him was different. His looks hadn't altered much—he looked older, of course, and there were a few strands of silver in his thick, floppy hair, and of course his body had…improved.

Riya had to pull her mind back from dwelling lovingly on those improvements. No, that wasn't it. In college he'd given the initial impression of being laid-back, slightly lazy, even, and that had been part of his charm—the fact that he never really exerted himself to make a good impression, but made one anyway. When she'd got to know him better, however, she'd figured that appearances were deceptive. The chilled-out exterior covered a lot of inner turmoil, the reasons for which, at seventeen, she hadn't even begun to understand. Now it seemed to be the other way around. Dhruv's personality was far more compelling, dynamic, but internally he seemed more detached than he'd been before, his wild streak completely dormant. Maybe he'd just grown up.

'I've grown up, too,' she informed the bedpost. 'I'm no longer a lovesick donkey. So there's no way I'm going to make a fool of myself over him again.'

The words were brave, but Riya felt about as confident as she had as a quaking four-year-old on her first day of school. Dhruv Malhotra meant trouble, and the less she saw of him the better.

CHAPTER TWO

GAURAV knocked gently on Riya's door. 'Come in!' she yelled out. He came in quietly and sat down, gingerly perching his bulky frame next to her.

'I'm sorry about foisting Dhruv on you,' he said, tugging gently at a lock of her hair. 'I wish I'd known—I wouldn't have asked him to stay here.'

'Relax. You're not a clairvoyant, so there's no way you could have known. It doesn't matter, anyway.'

'Should I ask him to move to a hotel? He's offered to, in case you're uncomfortable with him being around. Chutki's staying over at a friend's place from tonight anyway.'

Riya shook her head and laughed. 'It's not that big a deal, Gaurav. Really. Dhruv and I used to hang around in college—I took it a little too seriously and scared him off.'

Gaurav hesitated. '*He* seemed to think it'd be better if he moved out.'

'So let him move, then, for God's sake,' Riya snapped. 'It doesn't matter to me.' But it did. It mattered a lot. Chutki's saying that he'd held on to her picture had made her think that maybe, after all, Dhruv had cared for her—just a little. But if he still wanted to run away from her, even after twelve years, she couldn't help feeling some of the old hurt creep back.

Gaurav said gently, 'Do you want to tell me about it?'

Riya shook her head decisively. 'No, thanks. I made enough of a fool of myself over your cousin the first time around, and I don't want to think about it any more.'

'Poor girl.' Gaurav pulled her against himself for a quick hug. 'You know what? I think you guys should talk it over now, put it behind you.'

'Yeah, thanks for the advice, Oprah, but I think I'll pass.' The last thing she wanted was more time talking to Dhruv—it wouldn't be possible to conceal how much he affected her for more than ten minutes.

'Is it OK if he comes for my surprise party tonight?'

Riya groaned. 'Gaurav, you aren't supposed to *know* that there is a surprise party. Who blabbed?'

He gave her a smug grin. 'That's for me to know and you to find out… Come on, Riya, did you really think anything in the office would stay a secret?'

It didn't. Her office was the original leaky sieve—one of a dozen people could have told Gaurav, and she had been crazy to think that she'd be able to keep the surprise party actually a surprise.

'You can help clean the house before the party, then,' she told Gaurav, 'now that you know. Remember to put all your smelly socks in the wash.'

Gaurav groaned. 'I should have just pretended to be surprised. Like my grandmother says, there's no room for honesty in this black era. So, can Dhruv come?'

'I guess so,' Riya replied grudgingly, and he beamed back at her, evidently convinced that all was forgiven and forgotten between his cousin and his best friend.

* * *

The house was chock-full of people by eight p.m., and more kept arriving. Gaurav was popular in the firm, and because he was in HR he knew everyone. It was a bring your own booze party, and the food was Chinese takeaway and pizzas—it hadn't been much trouble to organise—but Riya was finding it difficult to concentrate even on simple things, like making sure someone responsible was in charge of the drinks, and that people didn't spill ketchup on the company-owned sofas. Her eyes automatically went to the door every time the doorbell rang—Dhruv had said he'd be late, but she couldn't help searching for him among every group of entrants.

It was nine-thirty when Dhruv finally made an appearance. Riya was perched on the balcony, swinging her legs against the parapet as she talked to a group of colleagues. The atmosphere in the room seemed to change as he walked in, looking around the room and hesitating a little before coming up to her. Riya gave him a polite, noncommittal smile, noticing bitterly that even with a day's stubble and rumpled clothes he was by far the best-looking man in the room.

As he walked towards her more than a few heads swung in his direction. The reaction in the little group on the balcony was palpable. The two women smoothed their hair, clearly in a bit of a flutter. Rishabh, the only man in the group, straightened up and squared his shoulders—the typical male reaction to a man several inches taller. Riya tried to stay unaffected, but she knew that she more than anyone else was conscious of every movement he made, every change of expression.

'So, what do *you* do, Dhruv?' one of the women asked after Riya had introduced Dhruv. 'Let me guess... Not a banker, obviously—not boring enough. Lawyer? Businessman?'

'I'm an architect,' Dhruv replied quietly.

'Really? What's your firm called?' Her expression was one of animated interest.

Dhruv, used to female attention, hardly noticed the effort she was making to capture his attention. It had been a long day, and he'd come back hoping for a relaxed evening, but with the house full of guests it didn't look likely. The woman was still looking at him expectantly, so he answered.

'Icarus Designs,' he said, wishing they would all go away and leave him with Riya. She was wearing a sleeveless turquoise top in some silky material over jeans, and her hair was loose over her shoulders—she looked younger, and far more as he remembered her from college, and if they had been alone he'd have been tempted to take her into his arms and kiss her senseless.

Rishabh looked up. 'There's a Singapore-based firm of that name—any connection?'

'I've been working out of Singapore the last few years, but I started in Delhi and I still have an office there,' Dhruv said. He had an eye on Riya, sensing that she was withdrawing from the conversation. He figured that while she was on friendly terms with Rishabh, she didn't really like him.

'Dude, I love the buildings you guys have done in Singapore,' Rishabh was saying. 'I worked in one of them, and the design was out of this world. I actually researched the firm as part of a project. Are you setting up something in Mumbai?'

'I'm considering it,' Dhruv said. 'I'll be coming back to Mumbai after Gaurav's wedding to scout for office space, and if things work out I'll set up here by the end of the year.'

Rishabh hopped down from the parapet onto the balcony and took a card out of his pocket. 'Maybe we can meet up once you're back? My contact details are on this—or I can call you if that's OK?'

'Sure,' Dhruv said, taking the card but not offering one of his own in return.

Riya frowned. It hadn't even occurred to her to ask Dhruv about his work, but Rishabh had sensed a business opportunity and honed in. That was how he managed to hold his own at work, she thought. They had joined CYB around the same time, and got along well at least on the surface, but professionally they had been at loggerheads since the day they'd started working together. Riya knew that she was technically far more competent than he was—where she fell behind was on the ability to spot new business.

She looked over the parapet, down at the city. She needed to get at least a couple of new clients on board this quarter to secure a decent bonus. God knew she needed the money. She earned a good salary, but a lot of it went home to her parents. Her mother didn't work, and her dad had retired on a very small pension—and he'd had a lot of health problems recently.

She pursed her lips worriedly. If Icarus Designs was big—and Rishabh evidently thought they were—*she* should speak to Dhruv about a possible project. He'd be far more inclined to talk to her than to Rishabh, but she felt very reluctant to broach the topic with him.

She cast a quick look in his direction, and all thoughts of work immediately flew out of her head. He was impossibly good-looking, she thought, confused, and his rumpled hair and unshaven chin only added to his dangerous bad-boy looks.

Dhruv looked up at her suddenly. 'Riya, don't lean

so far back—you'll topple. We're on the twenty-second floor.'

Gaurav walked up to them, drink in hand, slinging a careless arm around Dhruv's shoulders. 'Yeah, you'll make a lovely splat on the concrete. You guys heard the joke about the idiot who fell from the roof of a ten-storey building?'

Rishabh grinned—he and Gaurav were the clowns of the bunch. 'He heard the doorbell ring and ran to open the door.'

'Right. And the one who drove his truck off a cliff?'

'He wanted to check his air brakes!'

Dhruv moved closer to Riya and said in an undertone, 'Riya, please get down.'

She raised her eyebrows. 'Dhruv, I'm not about to fall. Back off.'

Rishabh said, 'And the one who fell out of the window?'

'He tripped over the cordless phone,' Gaurav said, grinning, as the girls groaned in mock exasperation.

Riya was still stubbornly perched on the balcony railing, giving Dhruv a defiant little look as she laughed at Gaurav's completely pathetic jokes. Dhruv had had these sudden bouts of over-protectiveness in college as well—worrying about her getting home when it was getting dark, insisting on dropping her home on his motorbike from college after she'd had an accident on her two-wheeler. She'd never objected then, thinking it was a sign of how much he cared for her, but there was no way she was going to take orders from him now.

'Don't be childish, Riya. What are you trying to prove?' he said, and Riya immediately saw red.

'Leave me alone,' she said.

Dhruv gritted his teeth and moved closer to her, putting one arm on either side in a protective stance.

'Get *away,* Dhruv,' Riya said angrily, not sure which was stronger—her irritation at his bossiness, or her intense awareness of his proximity. His sleeves were rolled up, and she could see the smattering of fine hair on his forearms. Her fingers ached to run up his arm, feel the muscles under the warm, velvety skin. His face was really close too, and she had a sudden mad impulse to touch his silky hair and pull his head closer till his mouth touched hers.

A surge of annoyance at her own susceptibility made her shove at his shoulder—hard. He didn't budge, but the movement made her lose her balance. She teetered on the edge for a second, and then Dhruv's arms came around her, steadying her and firmly lowering her to the balcony. His arms felt every bit as delicious as she had imagined. She looked up at him mistily—to encounter two golden eyes glaring furiously down at her as his hands came up to her shoulders.

He gave her a little shake. 'What did you think you were *doing*?' he demanded. His heart was still thudding loudly in his chest—for a moment he had really thought she was going to fall.

'I was perfectly OK till you tried to play the hero,' Riya retorted, shaking herself free from his clasp and storming off into her room.

Dhruv stared after her, a sense of déjà vu sweeping over him. The last time they'd spoken in college…

The circumstances had been very different, of course. Things had gone wrong between them, and he'd started cold-shouldering Riya, hoping she'd get the message and stay away from him. She hadn't stood for that very long, and had confronted him as he was leaving his hostel for a morning class. The altercation had turned bad very quickly. In the long years of hearing his parents fight he'd unconsciously acquired a knack of saying bitter, hurtful things, and it had taken him barely minutes to rip apart the delicate fabric of their relationship.

Riya's chin had gone up, and she'd said in a voice that was very firm, though tears were trembling on her long eyelashes, 'I don't believe you mean any of the nonsense you're saying, Dhruv. You're hurting yourself as much as you're hurting me, and that's just plain stupid.'

She'd turned and started walking away, and a blind wave of anger had ripped through him. He'd stretched out an arm and grabbed her, swinging her around against him. Her eyes had blazed up into his, and for a second he'd had a crazy impulse to crush her ridiculously childish little mouth under his. She'd felt very light against him, very fragile, and as he'd held her the fight had seemed to go out of her slim little body. He'd closed his eyes for a second, and then, very slowly, he'd released her, turning her away from him and pushing her gently back onto the path that led away from his rooms.

She'd turned back once to look at him as she walked away. If he'd made the smallest gesture he knew she'd have run back into his arms, but he'd kept his face blank, wiped clean of all expression and emotion. She hadn't looked back again.

Back in her room, Riya was thinking of the same morning, and the sense of utter desolation that had swept over her when she'd left Dhruv. A light tap on the door made her restrain herself from bursting into a flood of uncharacteristic tears.

'Come in,' she said gruffly.

Dhruv opened the door and stepped in, shutting it

behind himself. He sat down next to her and took her hand in both of his.

'I'm sorry,' he said softly. 'I overreacted. I have a bit of a thing about heights.'

Riya nodded, not trusting herself to speak. His hands were warm, slightly rough, and the temptation to fling herself into his arms was stronger than ever. Then a thought struck.

'You were OK with heights in college,' she remembered. 'You used to go on all those treks and things.'

Dhruv squeezed her hand slightly, and said after a brief pause, 'Yes, well, I'm not acrophobic. I saw a worker on one of my projects fall from the roof of a thirty-story building many years ago. Died instantly. I haven't been able to stand seeing anyone even lean out of a window since that.'

Riya's marshmallow heart immediately brimmed over with sympathy. 'That must have been terrible,' she blurted.

Dhruv shrugged, wishing he hadn't brought the subject up. It wasn't something he normally did—exposing vulnerability to win someone's sympathy. He hadn't done it consciously this time, either, but he'd felt a need to justify his behaviour. And not just his behaviour today. He looked away, pushing a hand through his hair. God, this was difficult. Seeing her walk away from him in anger today had brought back the guilt about how unfairly he'd treated her in the past, and he wasn't prepared to deal with it right now.

Riya felt her throat close up as she surveyed his back. The instant of sympathy she'd felt for him had temporarily breached her defences, and the old, confused sense of loss threatened to swamp her. She gritted her teeth and looked down for a second. She'd spent the day try-

ing to convince herself that she'd put the past behind
her, but who was she kidding? The past was right there,
waiting for her to let her guard slip, and the sooner she
figured out a way to deal with it the better.

'Dhruv?' she said finally, and he turned back to her.
'I never did get to ask you in college, but it's bothered
me all these years—why did you change?' Her heart
was pounding in her chest so hard that she could hardly
hear herself speak, but she couldn't stop herself continuing. 'I know I threw myself at you a bit at the end,
and you kept trying to knock some sense into me—
was that it?'

'Not really,' Dhruv said, and after a little pause he
continued very formally with a shuttered look on his
face that she remembered from college. 'I don't believe
in explanations, Riya—they always end up sounding
like excuses. But I do apologise. You deserved a lot better from me, and I let you down.'

The temptation to say more was almost irresistible,
but his reasons for dumping her were too closely linked
to the crisis his family had been going through at that
time. The old habits of reticence and concealment died
hard—even after so much time. It seemed preferable
that she think him fickle and irresponsible rather than
know the real reason.

'I'd better join the others—Gaurav looked like he
needed help with the food.' While Riya stared at him
in disbelief, he turned around and went out of the room,
shutting the door gently but firmly behind him.

'So much for waiting half a lifetime to figure out
what the hell happened,' Riya said out loud to the closed
door.

The sense of frustration was so strong she felt like
screaming. Twelve years since they'd parted, and expla-

nations still didn't seem to be among Dhruv Malhotra's strong points. In a way, she felt worse than she would have if he hadn't apologised—his getting angry or avoiding the topic would have made her feel that it really bothered him deep down, but the empty token of an apology relegated the whole college episode to an unfortunate but not very important incident in his distant past.

Suddenly furious, she picked up a little ceramic troll from her bedside table and hurled it across the room. It hit the wall and smashed into pieces with a most satisfying crash.

Her door opened a little, and Gaurav poked his head inside cautiously. 'All OK?' he asked.

Riya looked up and gave him a tight little smile. 'Yes. Your cousin is the…the most infuriating man I've met in my life—not that I care!' She didn't want to let Gaurav know quite how upset she was. He seemed to be fairly close to Dhruv, and given his general ineptitude at keeping his mouth shut the chances of him letting something slip were high.

Gaurav's pleasant face was creased with worry. 'He's leaving tomorrow, but he'll be there at the wedding. You sure it's OK?'

'I'll avoid him,' Riya said. And when Gaurav's frown didn't go away she said, 'Relax. I won't smash his face in during the ceremony. Or will it be simpler if I don't come?'

Gaurav's expression changed and he came in swiftly, sitting down next to her and saying earnestly, 'I wouldn't be getting married if you hadn't helped sort out things with Madhulika's parents. If anyone needs to skip the wedding, it'll be Dhruv.'

Sudden tears came to Riya's eyes, and she fumbled

for Gaurav's hand and squeezed it hard. He'd been her best friend for many years now, and he'd been miserable when Madhulika's parents had refused to let their daughter marry him. They'd picked out a Bengali bridegroom for her, and had had no time for the brash, burly Punjabi man their daughter had chosen. Riya had played the go-between for some months, gradually bringing them round to the idea, and Gaurav had been absurdly grateful ever since.

'Don't be silly,' she said. 'He's family—you can't tell him not to come. I promise I'll behave.'

'Come on out and join us, then,' Gaurav said, gently tugging her to her feet. 'I'm setting up the karaoke thing on the TV. Don't bother about Dhruv. Every unmarried girl in the room is making a beeline for him, and he'll be too busy fighting them off to bother you.'

Riya frowned as she followed Gaurav out. He was right—Dhruv was knee-deep in women, and in spite of herself she couldn't suppress a little flare of annoyance.

It was almost three in the morning when the last people left. Chutki had left for her friend's place at eleven, and Gaurav was dozing on the sofa. Riya started clearing up—there were beer cans and empty disposable plates and glasses scattered all over the room. Dhruv began to help, stacking boxes of half-eaten pizza and carrying them into the kitchen. She silently handed him a few garbage disposal bags, and picked up a broom and mop to clean the floor.

'Won't the maid do that tomorrow?'

'The place will be overrun by cockroaches by then,' Riya said. 'Armies of them come crawling in under the door if there's the slightest bit of food lying around.'

Gaurav looked at them sleepily. 'A cockroach can

live for a week without its head,' he informed them, and fell asleep quite suddenly, his mouth wide open.

Both Dhruv and Riya cracked up, the tension of the evening dissolving in gales of laughter.

'Let me get him to his room,' Dhruv said finally, and putting his arm around Gaurav, he half dragged him to bed.

Gaurav's room was a mess as well, but he decided not to do anything about it other than clear a couple of ashtrays off the bed before he headed back to the living room.

He was still undecided about Riya. One part of him felt that he should leave things as they were. The other would sell his soul to get within touching distance of her. His lips twisted as he acknowledged that, at present, the second was definitely winning.

After Riya had rejoined the party he'd spent the evening watching her unobtrusively as she circulated around the room, laughing and joking with people she obviously knew well. Little things had caught his attention and held it. The way she threw her head back when she laughed, exposing the long, perfectly shaped column of her throat. The way the silky material of her top clung to her body as she moved. The curve of her lush red lips betraying her amusement as she mock-frowned at something Gaurav said to her. He had never been so aware of a woman in his life. And now that they were finally alone in the room together it took every last ounce of his self-control to stop himself from dragging her into his arms and crushing her lovely mouth under his.

Oblivious to the direction Dhruv's thoughts were taking, Riya finished clearing the room and went to draw the curtains, groaning as she saw more mess on the balcony.

Dhruv came up behind her. 'I'll take care of that,' he said gently. 'Go to bed.'

'Why're you being so nice?' she demanded. Her voice came out sounding a little more petulant than she'd intended, and Dhruv's lips curved into his trademark sexy smile that started slowly at his mouth and went up all the way to his eyes. Riya's insides promptly turned to mush, in spite of her head telling her firmly to get a grip.

'We could forget college and try to be friends again,' he said, the words coming out before he had a chance to think. 'We'll be at the wedding for three days. We could use that time to catch up, get to know each other better?'

Riya closed her eyes briefly. It was such a tempting thought—getting to know Dhruv all over again. It would be stupid to deny that she was still strongly attracted to him—only she didn't know if he felt the same way, or if he was just trying to make amends for having hurt her earlier.

He was still looking at her expectantly. She forced a smile and said, as formally as she could, 'I guess we could try. I'm sorry if I've been less than gracious, Dhruv, but it's been a shock seeing you again. I thought I'd put all that nonsense from college behind me. Evidently it's still bothering me somewhere at some level, or I wouldn't have got so worked up when I saw you again.'

'I haven't managed to put it behind me, either,' Dhruv said softly. It seemed vital that he convince her to trust him—just a little. He took her hand and squeezed it gently. 'I don't think I expressed myself very well when we spoke earlier, but I truly am sorry I treated you the way I did. If you can forgive me for being such an idiot, let's spend some time together when we're in Kolkata. I swear I've improved with age.'

Riya looked into the familiar golden eyes for a second, and looked away hastily.

'OK,' she said, drawing her hand out of his warm clasp and brushing it clumsily across her forehead. 'I…I think I'll get to bed now. I'll see you tomorrow.'

The last lot of empty beer cans cleared away, Dhruv gave the kitchen a cursory glance before snapping off the light. Riya's reaction bothered him more than he cared to admit. Till the day they'd split up he had been used to Riya's adoration—she had concealed it under a layer of sassiness, but it had always been there. He hadn't expected it to remain, of course—not after so many years, and definitely not after the way they'd parted—but it was still a shock, looking into Riya's eyes and seeing wariness and distrust in their lovely depths. She was perfectly polite to him—only the genuine warmth that showed through when she spoke to Gaurav and even to Chutki was missing.

Regret and frustrated desire churned through him. Without realising it he'd had Riya captured in a timewarp in his mind, forever seventeen, forever willing and forever his. Rationally he knew that she'd have changed, but the reality of not having her come running when he beckoned was difficult to deal with.

He was about to go into the room Chutki had been using the night before when Riya's door opened again. She came out, wearing a white oversized T-shirt and little cotton shorts that left most of her long brown legs bare.

'I need a bottle of water,' she muttered, brushing past him to go into the kitchen and opening the fridge. Her throat was parched, and she hadn't been able to get to sleep, otherwise the last thing she'd have wanted was to run into Dhruv again. 'Great—someone drank all the cold water.'

She straightened up, and she looked so adorable with her wavy hair tousled around her sleepy face that Dhruv couldn't help pulling her close, all his good resolutions lost. She melted in his arms, closing her eyes as Dhruv trailed a finger down her cheek. His body tightened as he saw her reaction to him, and he lowered his lips slowly onto hers.

Dhruv's lips felt reassuringly familiar and wildly exciting at the same time, and Riya heard herself moan softly as she strained her body closer to his. The small part of her brain that was still functioning kept telling her that she was being stupid, only her body found it impossible to stop.

'You're so beautiful,' Dhruv said thickly, as his lips travelled down her neck and lower.

His hands were slipping under the loose T-shirt when Riya's brain finally kicked in.

'No,' she said. 'No, Dhruv…please, I need time to think.' And, grabbing the nearest bottle of *not* cold drinking water, she turned away and almost ran back to her room.

Riya was shaking as she sank down onto her bed. Another minute and they'd have been making love on the kitchen floor, oblivious of Gaurav sleeping in the next room. Or maybe that was just her. Going by past experience, Dhruv had probably had all his wits around him, however carried away he'd seemed. He'd probably thought it out fully—how they'd move to her room, make love the whole night through, and the next day he could pretend that nothing had happened. And, being the colossal fool that she was, she'd almost let it happen.

Slow tears began sliding down her cheeks. Of all things, she hated feeling vulnerable the most, and with Dhruv around all her carefully built armour was melting away.

Dhruv slowly turned off the lights in his room and got into bed. Kissing Riya had been a mistake—especially when she'd just started warming up to him. But it had been impossible to resist. The attraction between them had flared up as hot and sweet as it had so many years ago.

Dhruv had had several girlfriends since, and had thought he was fairly serious about at least two of them. It had been different with Riya, though. She was the first girl he'd ever kissed, one rain-soaked day at her home when her parents were away. Twelve years later he still remembered the feel of her eager, inexperienced lips under his, and her young body straining to be closer to him. It had taken every last ounce of sanity for him to leave her with just a kiss. She'd pouted and tried to pull him back, but he'd left anyway, muttering a hasty excuse. He hadn't trusted himself near her again, telling himself that he didn't need the added complication of a girlfriend in his already messy life.

He wasn't sure he wanted the complication in his life even now. He'd been thinking of settling down—his parents were pressing him to marry, and while he was cynical about their motives the idea made sense. None of his earlier girlfriends were the kind he'd want to marry—in the last twelve years he'd never met a woman he could imagine spending the rest of his life with. Which was one of the reasons why he'd even contemplated an arranged marriage. It had worked for several of his friends who lived overseas and didn't end up meeting too many Indian girls. Falling in love was a combination of hormones and stupidity in his view—his parents had supposedly married for love, and they had the worst relationship he'd ever seen.

After meeting Riya again, however, the thought of an arranged marriage seemed less appealing. The closest he'd come to falling in love had been with her. In the intervening years he'd tried to dismiss the episode as a piece of hormone-driven madness, but he knew it wasn't quite so simple. There was something between them that was very real, and while he didn't believe in love he had felt the absence of that spark in all his subsequent relationships.

The next day was less awkward than either Riya or Dhruv had anticipated. Gaurav hogged the limelight by waking up at ten when he had to catch a one-thirty flight, and announcing calmly over breakfast that he 'still needed to get his stuff together.' He panicked when Riya pointed out that as he'd need to be at the airport an hour before the flight, and it took forty-five minutes to get there, he had exactly an hour and a half within which to bathe, shave and pack for the wedding as well as the honeymoon.

In the ensuing flurry of activity to get Gaurav ready in time, Riya found herself and Dhruv slipping into a semblance of the easy camaraderie that had existed between them in the early days of their friendship.

'Why would you leave packing to the last minute?' Chutki moaned as she sat on a suitcase in an attempt to make it close.

'I thought I'd just need to take a couple of shirts and

jeans and the wedding *sherwani*,' Gaurav said in a harassed voice.

'And a few suits, and gifts for a dozen people, and clothes for the honeymoon,' said Dhruv, pulling a heap of boxes out of the cupboard where Gaurav had stacked and then conveniently forgotten about all the things he'd bought for the wedding. 'Not to mention the jewellery for Madhu. A psychoanalyst might think you *wanted* to miss the flight because of a deep-rooted subconscious phobia over marriage.' He took the suitcase from Chutki and, forcing the lid closed, snapped the clasps shut. 'Don't even *try* opening this till you reach Kolkata,' he warned, his deep voice betraying some of his affection for his cousin.

'No fear,' said Gaurav. 'It's full of girlie junk my mum bought for Madhu when she came to Mumbai. On *my* credit card, if I may add. By the way—I don't have a deep whatever you said marriage phobia.'

'I didn't say you did,' Dhruv retorted. 'I said a psychoanalyst might think that. A normal person would think you're an irresponsible idiot.'

Riya frowned at Dhruv, but then gasped as one of the boxes Gaurav was cramming into a second suitcase fell open to reveal a heavy gold necklace.

'You're mad, G-boy,' she said. 'I can't believe you left all this jewellery just lying around. What if we got burgled?'

'Ah, we wouldn't,' Gaurav said. 'I'm way too lucky for that. But I probably should have started packing earlier.' He slammed the last suitcase lid down and stood up, grinning at them proudly. 'All done.'

'He isn't going to make the flight,' Dhruv said flatly. 'Have you called for a cab, Gaurav?'

'Riya's going to drive us,' he said with an anxious glance towards her. 'Aren't you, Riya?'

She pretended to frown. 'Am I? I don't seem to recall you asking me.'

'Ah, Riya, sweetheart, please…' Gaurav went down on his knees. 'I'll be eternally grateful. Your slave for life. Please, *please* get me to airport—or I'll miss my wedding and my life will be ruined.'

'You're such a clown,' she said and, grabbing his hand, dragged him to his feet. 'Your wedding isn't for days. I'll drive you to the airport, though. One doesn't get promised eternal servitude every day.'

Gaurav threw his arms around her, hugging her exuberantly. She came out of his arms laughing, but stopped abruptly when she caught Dhruv's eye. There was a faintly condemning look on his face and she felt absurdly guilty.

Gaurav was probably her most favourite person outside her family. They had hit it off the day they met, and in spite of her initial awkwardness at sharing a flat with a man they had been best buddies ever since—to the extent that a lot of people thought they were related. Something about Dhruv's expression made her feel that he disapproved of her being so close to Gaurav, though—or at least that he disapproved of her hugging him.

The thought that he could be jealous crossed her mind, only to be dismissed immediately. She was reading too much into everything he said or did, she told herself firmly. It was about time she pulled herself together and started acting like a mature adult rather than a sixteen-year-old in the throes of her first crush.

'Maybe we should get the luggage loaded,' Dhruv said abruptly, cutting into her thoughts. 'Riya, come downstairs with me and show me where your car is parked.'

She nodded silently, wondering why she didn't object to him ordering her about. Dhruv had grabbed two of the heaviest suitcases, and his muscles rippled impressively under his tight-fitting T-shirt. Riya followed him to the door, dragging Chutki's wheeled bag behind her and trying not to ogle his perfectly shaped body too obviously.

'I'll bring the car up to the first floor, G-boy,' she called out as she shut the door. 'Be there in five minutes—Chutki, don't let him dawdle.'

'Chutki's a world champion dawdler herself,' Dhruv grunted as he put the suitcases down and hit the lift button. 'I'll be very surprised if they make it out of the flat before twelve.'

The lift was more than half full when it stopped at their floor, and there was only just about space for the two of them and the luggage. Riya had to squeeze in very, very close to Dhruv—and she was intensely conscious of the hard length of his body pressed against hers. If she moved her head a fraction her face would be buried in his chest, and she had to very firmly repress a desire to do just that. The scent of his woody cologne teased at her nostrils, and she was immensely relieved when the elderly lift finally made it to the ground floor, creaking noisily to a halt.

'This building needs some repairs,' Dhruv said as he stepped out. 'Decent construction, but very badly maintained. The stairwell's a garbage dump, too.'

'Shh, the secretary of the building society's just behind us,' Riya hissed, not sure whether she was more annoyed at his rudeness or about the fact that he had been thinking about the condition of the stairwell when she had been busy lusting after his near-perfect body.

Dhruv shrugged. 'So?' he asked. 'I'm sure he's noticed that the building's about to fall down, and if he hasn't, it's about time someone pointed it out to him.'

'Lots of buildings in Mumbai are like that,' Riya retorted over her shoulder as she marched off towards her car.

She'd bought a spanking new, bright red Hyundai i10 a few months back, and was intensely proud of it—in spite of the niggling feeling that she shouldn't have spent so much money on herself when her parents were so hard up. Gaurav had held off buying his own car because the flat came with only one parking space, and in return she chauffeured him around whenever he wanted, and nobly refrained from retaliating when he made remarks about her somewhat reckless driving.

'Is this it?' Dhruv asked in disbelief as she used the button on her keychain to remotely unlock the car. 'Where does the luggage go? The car doesn't have a trunk.'

'Of course it does,' Riya said crossly, swinging up the back. 'The luggage goes right here. And what's left of it goes in the rear seat.'

'Well, I'm sitting in front, then,' Dhruv said decisively, opening the passenger door and moving the seat back to accommodate his long legs. 'Who's this car made for? Under-eights?'

Riya slammed her own door shut with a very final thud. 'Don't you dare insult my baby, Dhruv Malhotra,' she said firmly. 'Otherwise you may just find yourself chucked out on the road halfway to the airport if McQueen decides he doesn't like you.'

Dhruv's lips twitched. 'Is that its name? Wouldn't a car be female?'

'Only if it belonged to a dumb male,' Riya said, backing out of the parking lot and speeding up the ramp to stop in front of the first floor lobby.

Gaurav and Chutki were nowhere in sight, and it was drizzling slightly so she couldn't get out of the car. Stuck in a confined space with Dhruv, she was even more conscious of the sheer animal attraction of the man. He was probably thinking about trusses and beams again, though, she thought as she saw him look up at the building critically.

'About last night...' he began slowly.

Riya rushed into speech. 'Let's forget about it, shall we?' she said. 'I think we both got a little carried away.'

'"A little" being an understatement,' Dhruv murmured, but he let it drop. Riya reminded him of a high-spirited but nervous filly, shying away whenever he got too close. She hadn't been that way when he first knew her, nor had she been so worried about appearances. He'd picked up on the way she'd carefully tried to hide any hint of the conflict between them from Chutki, from the guests at the party last night, even to an extent from Gaurav. Twelve years ago she wouldn't have cared who knew about it if she was upset with him.

'So the car's a favourite, is it?' he asked her, and she immediately brightened up as the conversation moved to neutral ground.

'Yes,' she said, looking adorably embarrassed. 'It's my first car. Actually, it's the first car in my family— my parents had a scooter, and my sister uses a two-wheeler, too.'

Dhruv nodded. Most people in small towns used two-wheelers, cars being reserved only for the well-to-do. His family had always owned a car, though, and his own first car hadn't been a novelty—just a set of wheels to get him from one place to another.

He gave Riya a slow, sexy smile, and her insides promptly turned to mush. It was positively sinful the way the man could turn her on with just a look, she thought despairingly. His proximity was like a drug, slowly dulling her instincts for self-preservation.

Dragging her eyes away from his, she spotted Chutki and Gaurav coming out of the foyer loaded with luggage. 'There they are,' she said in relief. Any more time with Dhruv and she'd do something stupid—the more people around the better. Ideally, she'd have liked him to move to the back seat, as even with Chutki and Gaurav there she was intensely aware of his closeness, of his knee almost touching hers, his arm loosely slung around the back of his seat as he turned to speak to Gaurav.

Riya drove off the second Gaurav and Chutki had loaded the remaining luggage and got into the car, barely giving Gaurav time to shut the door. He normally teased her about her driving—today, though, he had reason to thank her for her careless disregard for speed limits. They made it to the airport barely ten minutes before the check-in counter closed. She got out of the driver's seat to help load the suitcases onto two trolleys.

'See you in a couple of days,' she said to Gaurav, and hugged him hard, giving Dhruv a slightly defiant look, as if to tell him he could take his disapproval and shove it.

Chutki hugged her, too, saying breathlessly, 'Thanks a million, Riya. Crazy driving, girl.'

Dhruv was standing next to her, and he touched her hand briefly. 'Thank you for getting us here in one piece,' he said. 'I'll see you at the wedding.'

The feel of his hand sent a little tingle of sensation up Riya's arm, and she felt her heart do a dutiful little flip-flop inside her chest when he smiled at her. She wanted to hold on to his hand, but she managed to step back, waving to the three of them as they went into the departure terminal.

The next day was Monday, and Riya dragged herself to work with more than the normal amount of reluctance. She'd spent the night dreaming embarrassingly erotic dreams about Dhruv, and she wanted to get right back into bed and continue dreaming them. She'd finally convinced her very reluctant self that she needed to steer clear of him, and the dreams were a kind of consolation prize to make up for renouncing the real thing. Especially the ones in which he took off his clothes. Of course her imagination had to supply a fair bit there, given that she'd never actually seen him naked. For all she knew the dreams were *better* than reality, and they had the advantage of no embarrassing mornings after.

Grumpily getting into the office half an hour late, she found that the finance team had decided to assert their importance by rejecting a proposal she'd sent them the previous Thursday. The first half of the day was spent fighting a royal battle with them, and second half went in convincing a client not to ditch them and go with someone else.

Riya was bushed by the time she got home. The landline was ringing when she let herself in, and she dropped her laptop on her toes in her hurry to pick it up.

'Good evening, CYB. Riya Kumar speaking,' she said.

There was a pause, and then an amused male voice said, 'I thought this was your home number?'

'Damn. Yes, it is. I'm just so used to answering my desk phone at work. Sorry, who's this?'

'Dhruv.'

Riya's heart did its little pitter-patter number again as she strove to simultaneously keep her voice under control and stop herself from saying anything stupid. 'Oh,' she said lamely at last. 'Hi.'

'Hi,' he replied, his spirits rising absurdly high at the sound of her voice. He'd spent the whole day thinking about her almost constantly, and about arranged marriages, and had decided that whatever he had with her needed to be fully explored before he committed to life with a stranger. It might not end up being anything more than a short fling, but even that would give him a chance to work the powerful attraction he felt for her out of his system.

'When are you reaching Kolkata, Riya?' he asked.

'Um, around ten a.m. on Wednesday, I think,' she said guardedly. She wasn't sure why he was asking, and she had a bad feeling about where this conversation was going.

'I'll come and pick you up, if that's all right? We're in the same guest house, and I've hired a driver for the week. I thought we could go round the city a bit—Gaurav and Madhu will be busy with wedding preparations, and we only need to be at the engagement party at eight.' Then, as she hesitated, 'Just one day, Riya. There's no harm in that, is there?' He was careful to keep his voice as platonically friendly as possible, not wanting to scare her off.

No harm, a little imp prompted in Riya's brain. *No harm at all.*

She squished the imp firmly. No imp was going to tell her when and how to make a fool of herself over a man who'd already done his best to break her heart once. On the other hand, the imp had a point. Maybe if she spent some time with Dhruv she'd find that she'd been fooling herself all along, and that she didn't really like the man.

Her tongue sprang into action before she had time to complete the thought. 'OK,' she said. 'Only...look, I'm not trying to be rude, but I don't want you to get the wrong impression. I'm really, really not in the market for a random fling right now. In spite of all the dumb things I did that night.'

'I'm not rushing you into anything,' Dhruv said, trying to maintain his calm and platonic approach, though the thought of spending several days with Riya without touching her sounded like a not very refined kind of torture. Something that an old-time sage of the Rishi Vishwamitra variety might cook up, meditating in solitary splendour while scantily clad nymphs danced around him.

The distracting thought of Riya in an apsara costume crossed his mind, and he desperately tried to dispel the image from his head. 'You said you wanted time to think, and I respect that.'

'Well, I've thunk. I mean, I've thought,' she said, getting irritated both with him and herself. 'Being friends is fine, but I don't want to get into any kind of a physical relationship with you. And before you say it, I *know* it's quite as much my fault as yours. I am planning to exercise extreme levels of self-control, and I hope you can do the same.'

The amusement back in his voice, Dhruv said, 'Can do. OK if I pick you up, then?'

'Yes,' Riya said grudgingly, and put the phone down, hating how easily he'd agreed. He at least could have *pretended* to be a little upset at the thought of having to exercise self-control, she thought crossly to herself. Or at least pretended that he would *need* to exercise some self-control.

Of course he'd probably had a spectacular sex life the last few years. Dozens of women could have been queuing up to sleep with him in Singapore for all she knew. She'd only *almost* lost her virginity once, in a disastrous encounter with her almost-fiancé, and the experience had been enough to put her off the thought of sex for years. It had also been enough for her to break off her almost-engagement with Vinay.

Dhruv was different. Even at twenty he had known what he was doing, and their short clinch in the kitchen showed that he'd only improved with age. Sex with him would be…an educative experience—and if she were sure that she could trust herself not to fall for him again she'd have let her inhibitions go hang and plunged into an affair with him.

Riya grinned unwillingly to herself at how attractive that proposition sounded. She wasn't hardboiled enough to go through with it, though. At some point her emotions would get thoroughly involved, and there was no way she could afford to let that happen.

CHAPTER THREE

DHRUV was waiting for her at the airport, and Riya's carefully built up composure nearly crumbled at her first sight of him. He was wearing old jeans and a white cotton shirt, and his hair was still a little damp from the shower. He looked good enough to eat. The first two buttons of the shirt were open, exposing a triangle of golden skin that she couldn't take her eyes off. Her fingers ached to reach out and touch him. She tried to tell herself again that he was a shallow, heartless man who was out for a good time and didn't really care about her getting hurt in the process, but her heart wasn't in it. *Who cares if he's out for a good time?* the imp in her head said impatiently. *And what's wrong with a good time anyway?*

And what kind of idiot agreed to a day-long date with the hottest man she'd ever known and then told him that she didn't want him to touch her? What was the *point of* a hot man if he was going to be physically out of bounds? What was she? Some kind of modern-day Puritan, trying to suppress the evil call of the flesh?

'Good flight?' Dhruv asked, completely unconscious of her inner tussles as he took her bag from suddenly nerveless fingers.

She nodded, giving herself a little mental shake and

looking away from him. Dhruv seemed completely un-affected by her, she noticed bitterly as he strode away towards the car. Evidently she needed to work a lot harder on her reactions to him—he seemed completely comfortable with the platonic let's-get-to-know-each-other-again-and-not-try-to-rip-off-each-other's-clothes rule that she'd set earlier.

Kolkata was utterly unlike what Riya had expected it to be. Even in the general haze of lust that seemed to surround her in Dhruv's company she managed to no-tice enough to interest her. Her impressions of the city had been formed partly by the stories she'd heard from the Bengali neighbours she'd had growing up, and partly from Dominique Lapierre's *City of Joy,* and the state-liness of the old parts of the city took her by surprise.

They spent some time walking up and down College Street, browsing through second-hand books, and had lunch at a quaint little restaurant off Park Street. Riya wasn't sure if Dhruv was aware of the effect he had on her—if he was, then the casually friendly tone he'd ad-opted with her was nothing short of deliberate torture. If he wasn't—a depressing thought—then maybe he'd meant what he said about just wanting to spend a day with her while they went around the city. Maybe his kissing her that night had been an impulse, and he was trying to convey a subtle message that he didn't want to take things any further. He definitely did seem far more interested in the buildings than in her—true to his promise, he hadn't touched Riya even once—but he was so tantalisingly close that as far as Riya was concerned extreme self-control had to be exercised al-most constantly.

They were wandering around the grounds of the Victoria Memorial when Dhruv's phone rang. It was a short conversation, and he was frowning when he rang off.

'Everything OK?' Riya ventured. She hadn't understood much because he'd been speaking in Marathi—she was a little surprised that he was so fluent. She'd been living in Maharashtra for many years and could barely string two sentences of the local language together.

'Yes,' he said still frowning. 'It was my mother—she decided not to come to Kolkata for the wedding, but she's been calling every few hours to check on what's happening.'

Riya looked up, for a second distracted from her absorption in the man next to her. It was odd, she realised, his parents not coming for Gaurav's wedding. Her own parents went to every wedding in the family. Even a second cousin twice removed counted as family. They skimped and saved for gifts, travelling second class by train to get to the wedding. Some of her best memories as a child were of those weddings, watching her mother all decked out in one of her three silk saris, playing with cousins she hadn't met since the last relative's wedding, proudly handing over the elaborately wrapped gift to the bride.

'Why isn't she coming?' she asked finally.

'Long story,' Dhruv said. He hesitated a little before continuing—he was still reluctant to talk about his family, but he was making a conscious effort to be less secretive than he'd been in the past. 'Gaurav's my cousin on my dad's side, and my mother doesn't get along with a lot of the relatives who are coming for the wedding. She's Maharashtrian—my dad was the first Malhotra to marry a non-Punjabi, and my grandparents were not thrilled, to put it mildly. The whole extended family went out of their way to give her a tough time the first few years. Mum still hasn't got over it, and she avoids meeting them when she can. But, anyway, she's pretty close to Gaurav, and now she's feeling bad that she didn't make it.'

'Is your father coming?' She felt immediate sympathy for Dhruv's mother, but missing the wedding because of some decades-old feud seemed extreme—and also unfair to Gaurav.

Dhruv shook his head. 'He'd get asked a lot of questions if he came without Mum. He's made some excuse, saying that he can't get away from work right now.'

He fell silent, and Riya instinctively changed the topic. 'What projects are you working on currently?' she asked.

Dhruv shrugged. 'Lots of them. Some office complexes, a stadium in Malaysia, a low-cost housing project in India… I don't really do much designing now; I'm more involved with the business side of things.'

'But I thought the whole point of having your own firm was that you could do the kind of work you liked,' Riya said. 'What do you do all day, then, if you're not designing buildings?'

'I still work on some of them. But my partner, Krish, is the creative genius behind our work. I'm the guy who goes out and gets us the projects. And we've built a name for ourselves, so that part is getting easier—we work with some of the biggest construction companies in Southeast Asia, and there's a lot of repeat business.'

He'd changed, Riya thought, struggling to reconcile a Dhruv who spent all his time pitching projects with the man she remembered. He'd been in love with his work then, full of ideas on how he'd transform Indian cityscapes if he had the chance.

Some of her confusion must have shown on her face, because Dhruv said, 'Krish is amazing—you should see some of his designs. I realised within a few months of working with him that I wouldn't ever be as good as him, no matter how hard I tried.'

He'd come to terms with it quickly, adjusting their workload so that he managed clients and left Krish free to work on his own ideas. And when the ideas needed tweaking—either to fit a budget or to satisfy an egotistical client's need to have a say in what finally got built—he did the work, modifying the design to please the client without losing the essence of what Krish had created.

'Don't look so horrified, Riya,' he said, lightly touching her hand. 'I know everyone in college thought I was a genius, but in the wider scheme of things I'm a better businessman than an architect.'

That had been a far more galling realisation—that after all his contempt for his Punjabi money-grubbing father, his own strengths were in the same area. The firm had barely kept its head above water under Krish—he'd rejected too many projects because he couldn't get along with the client, and he was terrible at ensuring that money owed to him was paid. Within a year of Dhruv's joining Icarus had been safely in the black, and now they raked in so much that neither Krish nor Dhruv really knew what to do with the money.

Riya still didn't look convinced, but something about Dhruv's expression warned her not to probe too deep. It was as if he had invisible 'No Entry' signs posted all around him.

'Do you miss India?' she asked finally.

He shook his head. 'Not really. Singapore is a good city to live in, and my work brings me to India often enough. How about you—have you ever thought of emigrating?'

'I worked in the Manhattan office of CYB for around a year. It was exciting, but I don't regret having come back,' Riya said, too embarrassed to admit that she'd missed her family so much she'd cut the assignment short to come home. 'I like travelling, but I don't like the thought of living overseas. Mumbai's big and dirty and crowded and smelly, but I love it all the same,' she said, making Dhruv laugh. 'I wouldn't move anywhere else for the world.'

It was drizzling when they finally left the Victoria Memorial, and Riya turned her face up to the rain. Dhruv slung an arm over her shoulder as they walked to the car, and the atmosphere between them changed imperceptibly.

Riya stopped trying to puzzle out Dhruv's character, intensely conscious of his nearness, and Dhruv tensed, wondering if she'd run scared. He'd been very careful all day to stick to her no-touching rule—at least in spirit. He hadn't been able to resist touching her casually a few times, and now his self-control was stretched to breaking point. She didn't seem to be resisting his nearness now, and in the car he pulled her closer. Riya went to him, putting a head on his shoulder almost against her will. She knew she wasn't being sensible, but suddenly she didn't care. To hell with over-analysing her own feelings, she thought. This was here and now, and it didn't matter if they never spoke to each other again. His arms around her were proof of the fact that he wasn't as indifferent to her nearness as he'd pretended to be all day.

It was almost night, and in one of the dark stretches between lampposts he bent down and brushed his lips lightly, almost casually across hers. 'This no-touching rule isn't working, is it?' he whispered softly into her ear. 'I can't keep my hands off you.'

Riya didn't reply, but she kissed him back in the next dark stretch, her teeth nipping at his mouth so hard that she drew blood, the salt taste unfamiliar and exciting on her tongue. He pulled her against him, burying his face in her hair and nibbling at the nape of her neck as their driver sped the car through near-empty streets.

In the guest house, Dhruv walked her to her room. She had trouble opening the padlock on the door, the key finally slipping from her hands down to the floor. He picked it up and opened the door for her silently. They were already late for the cocktail party, and he was turning away to go back to his room when Riya impulsively pulled him inside. He said softly, half-protestingly, 'Riya…' and then she was in his arms.

His lips touched hers gently at first, then a little more urgently. She completely lost control as his tongue slipped into her mouth, flinging her arms around him and moaning softly. His arms tightened around her as he backed her against the door—they were both flushed when they pulled apart a minute later. He looked as dazed as she felt, but he put her away from him gently.

'I should leave now,' he said.

His shirt was unbuttoned almost to his waist—Riya must have done that at some point, though she had no recollection of anything other than the sensation of his mouth on hers. Dhruv started buttoning it with shaky fingers, and then stopped abruptly to pull her into his arms again. It was almost killing him to back away from her now, but he knew that he couldn't take advantage of the moment of weakness that had made her melt into his arms. She didn't trust him yet, and she never would if he allowed things to go any further. It was hard to let her go, though, and he held her in his arms for a long, long moment.

'You can't pretend this doesn't exist, Riya,' he whispered into her hair.

'I'm not pretending it doesn't,' she said slowly. 'I find you madly attractive. I always did. And I know you're doing your best, but my plan to exercise extreme self-control isn't working even with me. When I think with my head, though—' she started doing up the remaining buttons on his shirt '—which admittedly I don't do very often when I'm around you… I'm sorry,' she said, as he groaned softly in response to her wayward hand slipping inside his shirt to do some independent investigation of its own. 'Well, I think we should take things a little more slowly, that's all.'

The corners of Dhruv's mouth quirked up. 'I see. So are we back to the no-touching rule?' he asked, looking pointedly at her hands, which were now at the waistband of his jeans.

Riya stepped back from him hastily, putting her hands behind her back. 'Um, maybe not a no-touching rule, exactly. I mean, we're kind of beyond that stage, I guess.'

'I guess,' he replied seriously, with only a little hint of a smile lurking in the corner of his eyes. 'What do you suggest we do, then?'

'Um, I don't know…' Riya stumbled a little over her words. 'Take things as they come? Basically, what I'm saying is,' she said in a hurried rush of words, 'we shouldn't sleep together until we're sure where we're going with this whole thing. I mean, I know you've been living overseas, and sex isn't such a big thing there, and I'm not a virgin, either—at least not technically—but

I'm still a little…' Her eyes wandered to the clock and she gave a little yelp of alarm. 'Dhruv, it's already past eight! The party!'

'Relax,' he said, now sounding more amused than ever. 'Nothing will start before nine.' He bent his head and gave her a hard kiss, murmuring, 'We'll talk after the party—meet you downstairs in ten minutes.'

He strode from the room.

Riya spent most of the ten minutes trying to gather her scattered wits as she scrambled into the outfit she'd bought for the party. It was too late to do anything with her hair, so she piled it up on her head, securing it with a diamanté clasp and letting a few tendrils escape around her neck. Hoping that the end result looked carelessly stylish as opposed to simply careless, she grabbed her clutch and hurried out into the foyer.

Dhruv was checking his e-mails. 'Let's go. Are we *very* late?' Riya asked as she ran into the room.

Her voice broke off, and a charming wave of colour flooded her face as Dhruv looked up, his eyes widening in appreciation as he took in the slightly off-the-shoulder *kameez,* with a beaded bodice that clung lovingly to her breasts, and the skin-tight *churidaar* that showed off her long, shapely legs. A chiffon *dupatta* covered her almost bare shoulders, the deep cream colour perfectly offsetting her dusky skin. He didn't say anything though, letting his eyes do the talking.

They were both silent in the car during the drive, though Dhruv took her hand into a reassuringly warm clasp, releasing it only when they reached their destination.

The party was at a South Calcutta club, and Gaurav was looking a little ill at ease as he stood talking to a few of his future father-in-law's friends. He hailed Riya and Dhruv with relief, politely excusing himself from the retired senior civil servant who'd been haranguing him on the latest populist budget.

'Thank heavens you guys are here,' he muttered in an undertone. 'I've been trying to convince these guys for hours that I work in HR and I know squat about finance—' He broke off as he took a good look at Riya. '*Arre,* sex-bomb! Let me take a look at you…' He grabbed her shoulders, and pulled Riya around to look at her properly. 'Man, you clean up pretty good. Who'd have thought it, seeing you in those ancient track-pants you wear around the flat?'

An elderly couple who'd just come in heard him and backed away, looking scandalised.

'You might want to lower your voice a little,' Dhruv said drily. 'You don't want the guests thinking you're a dirty old man.'

Gaurav gave him a look. 'I need a drink. And, by the way, Seema Chachi's looking all over the place for you.'

Dhruv grimaced. 'I know. I've been trying to avoid her. *Chalo,* I need a drink, too. Should I get you something, Riya?'

Riya shook her head. 'No, thanks.'

She was looking around for someone she knew when Chutki bounced up to her.

'Where's Dhruv got to?' she asked. 'I thought I saw him with you a minute ago.'

'He's with Gaurav—they're trying to avoid some aunt of yours.'

Chutki grinned her funny lopsided little grin. 'All these aunties are going crazy, trying to line up girls for Dhruv to meet,' she confided. 'He's in India for only two weeks, and he's met three of them in Nagpur and two in Kolkata, and there are some ten lined up in

Delhi, and another six in Bombay. I'm getting to short-list the Delhi and Bombay ones now, as there's no way he'll have time to meet all of them.'

Riya felt as if she'd been slapped in the face. 'He's looking to get married?' she asked in a voice that didn't sound like her own.

Chutki nodded. 'Mum's been having a go.'

After the initial shock, Riya wondered cynically why she was so surprised. Finding a bride was usually one of the top items on a homecoming non-resident Indian's to-do list, given the lack of fair, virginal and house-wifely Indian girls overseas. And it wasn't as if he'd made any promises to *her*. Maybe she'd even figured somewhere on his list of prospective brides—probably fairly low down, given her dusky complexion and lack of housewifely qualities. And she'd have slid even further down—if not off the list altogether—with her en-thusiastic response to his kissing.

'Aren't your parents doing the short listing?' Riya asked finally, when the silence had stretched out long enough for Chutki to begin looking at her curiously. 'Of the girls, I mean?'

'Nope, my dad's too busy, and Mum doesn't get along too well with the relatives on my dad's side. Aunty Seema's managing the whole thing. Dad wanted him to start off meeting Punjabi girls and Mom got bugged—*she'd* been checking out all these fair Cobra girls on matrimonial websites. Konkanastha Brahmin,' she ex-plained, seeing Riya's puzzled look. 'It's the cub-caste my mum belongs to. Not the cobras you find in the Alipore zoo. So, anyway, Aunty Seema's in charge now.'

Riya raised her eyebrows. 'Surely Dhruv has a say in choosing who he wants to marry?'

'He does,' Chutki said slowly. 'It's just that he's had

dozens of girlfriends, and... Never mind. I'm talking too much as usual.' A relative came up to speak to her, and Riya took the opportunity to slip away quietly while Chutki was distracted.

Gaurav and Madhulika came upon Riya an hour later, sitting in a corner, carefully nursing her seventh alcopop. She gave Gaurav a brilliant smile, and he immediately asked suspiciously, 'How many of those have you had?'

'Two of each flavour,' she said happily. 'And very nice they were!'

Gaurav stared at Madhu in consternation. 'She's sloshed.'

'She can't be, Gaurav, those things are really mild. Even a child of two couldn't get drunk on them—they're like fizzy fruit juice.'

'I don't know about a child of two. I've seen this child of twenty-nine get high on a single Bloody Mary. Not everyone can knock back vodka shots like you, Madhu.'

'Not sloshed,' Riya said firmly, and stood up and walked towards them very carefully. 'Can walk.'

'How many flavours does this stuff come in, anyway?' Gaurav asked exasperatedly, as he tried to stop Riya from bumping into a waiter carrying a stack of glasses.

'Three, I think,' Madhu said, giggling. 'Orange, lime, cranberry—or, no. Four. There's one more—pineapple or something.'

'Mango,' Riya said, frowning slightly. 'That's what I'm drinking now. It's...'

'Nice,' completed Gaurav. 'I know. You told us before. Let me get hold of Dhruv. Someone needs to take you back to the guest house.'

'You got Gaurav really worried,' Dhruv said in the car, reaching out to tuck a strand of hair behind Riya's ear.

She shook her head crossly, away from his hand. 'He's turning into a fussy old woman,' she said. 'Nag, nag, all the time. Who knows what Madhulika sees in him? He isn't even good-looking. Looks like a Teletubby.'

Dhruv laughed. 'Aren't you being a little mean?' he asked.

'I'm not mean,' Riya said indignantly. 'Imagine sleeping with a tub of lard like that. Poor Madhu. I shouldn't have helped her marry him. She'll get squashed on the first night and it'll be all my fault.'

She looked genuinely perturbed, and Dhruv stopped trying to reason with her. He'd seen enough drunk people in his life, but Riya drunk was as unique as Riya sober.

He took her to her room and, taking the key from her, unlocked the door. She walked across the room and flopped into bed fully dressed. Dhruv gently tugged her *dupatta* away and hung it over the back of a chair before he left the room, shutting the door gently behind him. She looked like a little kid, he thought, in spite of the sophisticated clothes, and he felt suddenly protective—though he realised ruefully that the only thing she needed protecting against right now was *him*.

Riya stared into the darkness for a long time after he left. The effects of the alcohol had worn off during the drive back, and she'd been acting drunk after that to stop Dhruv from talking to her. Tears welled into her eyes. It was ridiculous how susceptible she was to him—and how easily he could hurt her even without trying. He'd probably be bewildered if he knew that she was upset at the thought of him meeting a line-up of prospective brides, and she couldn't blame him. He'd made no promises to her, no commitments, only asked for some time together to get to know each other. A request that she was now almost a hundred percent sure she should have refused.

She turned towards the wall, tears welling up in her eyes again. So much for trying to act like a sophisticated woman of the world. She was still the stupid lovesick girl she'd been in college, and the quicker she accepted it the better.

The next morning Dhruv glanced at his watch as he sipped his coffee. It was almost ten, and there was no sign of Riya yet. A bunch of her colleagues from CYB had arrived on the morning flight from Mumbai and were chattering loudly around the breakfast table. One girl was giving him flirtatious looks, and Dhruv had carried his coffee into the foyer to get away from her. He glanced at his watch again. *Damn,* he'd hoped to be able to talk to Riya before they had to leave for the *haldi* ceremony.

The morning wasn't going well. Aunty Seema had called him to say that she'd lined up two girls in Kolkata for him to 'meet'—one of them was supposed to be at the wedding in the evening. He'd had to tell her that he wasn't interested in meeting anyone, and she'd asked a lot of awkward questions.

Dhruv sighed. In Singapore the thought of an arranged marriage had seemed practical enough. He was thirty-two, and so far hadn't met anyone he liked well enough to settle down with. His parents, for once united on something, were insisting he marry and, tired of bachelor life, he had agreed. His views on marriage had changed a lot over the years—with far more experience of the world he now saw his parents' marriage in proper perspective: not as the personal calamity it had appeared to be when he was younger, but the natural outcome when two people with irreconcilable differences forced themselves to live together.

He hadn't bargained for Riya's reappearance in his life, though. He still distrusted strong emotions, but the physical chemistry between the two of them was something he no longer wanted to fight. The attraction between them was stronger than anything he'd ever felt before, and he'd begun to think that marriage without a spark of that sort would be a dull and soulless affair.

'Going with the flow,' as Riya had suggested, seemed to be a good option. His lips twitched as he remembered her confusion the day before, and her explanation that she was 'technically' not a virgin. She'd almost got married once, Gaurav had told him—not surprising, really. What was more surprising was that she was currently unattached. Out of choice, Gaurav had said. She had her fair share of admirers—some of them extremely eligible. Dhruv felt his stomach muscles clench as an unfamiliar surge of jealousy overcame him. Several men had been eyeing her at the party the day before, and he'd had to firmly suppress a purely primitive urge to walk across and rearrange their faces for them.

It was after ten by the time Riya finally came down, and two of her CYB colleagues were with her. Dhruv looked up with a teasing smile. 'Feeling better now?' he asked.

She nodded and slid into a chair next to him, reaching for a plate of *idlis*. It was true. She'd finally fallen into a dreamless sleep, and had woken in the morning feeling far more well equipped to think rationally.

'Are you leaving for the *haldi* ceremony right away?'
Dhruv asked.

'I guess so. Aren't you?'

Dhruv shook his head. 'There's some stuff I need
to finish.'

Probably going off to interview a few candidates for
his hand, Riya thought nastily, hoping they turned out
to be really horrible. She waved goodbye to him cheerfully enough, though, and then dug out a little scrap
of paper from her bag to look at the list she'd made in
the morning.

Dhruv Malhotra: Pros and Cons the heading said.

Cons:
Prone to sudden dumping without explanation
Way out of league looks-wise
Way out of league moneywise
Way out of league in pretty much all ways
Is planning an arranged marriage
Pros
Wonderful sex?

She thought over it for a while, chewing her lower
lip, and then scratched out the question mark after 'wonderful sex'. That wasn't the area where the doubts were.
Making lists usually helped her sort out things in her
mind—they always had—but this one wasn't doing its
job properly. She still wasn't sure whether she should
tell Dhruv that she didn't want to spend any more time
with him, or stick with her original plan of 'going with
the flow'. Sighing, she tore up the list and went upstairs
to get ready.

Gaurav's *haldi* ceremony was in a flat his parents had
rented for the wedding. The flat was crowded with noisy

relatives, and there were bright yellow turmeric streaks all over the furniture.

'You look like you're in the last stages of jaundice,' Riya told Gaurav critically. 'Put a shirt on, for God's sake. Aren't they done with you yet?'

He shook his head mournfully as yet another girlishly giggling aunt attacked him with a handful of turmeric paste.

'It'll never wash off,' Chutki said solemnly. 'You'll have to get married looking like a demented mango.'

Gaurav's mother looked up. 'Come—you girls must be getting bored here. Chutki, take Riya up to the terrace and show her the view,' she said. 'Take something to eat with you.'

The view was good—though Riya suspected that Mrs Khanna had sent them there to get rid of them. Chutki had carried up a little plate of biscuits, which she was now examining carefully.

'They look like dog biscuits,' she pronounced crossly. A tall bronzed man stepped onto the terrace, and Chutki abandoned the biscuits with a little squeal. 'Karan!' she screamed excitedly, and she flung her arms around her brother.

Riya looked at him with interest. Dhruv had mentioned in passing that his younger brother was a wildlife photographer. Karan was not as good-looking as Dhruv, but his appearance was as striking. His features were uneven, and he was dark—much darker than his brother, even under the tan he'd acquired in his outdoor job. His hair was cropped very, very short, and the tail of a dragon tattoo peeped out from under the sleeve of his black shirt. But he had an interesting face—like Dhruv, he was the kind of man who would stand out in a crowd.

Chutki dragged him over to introduce him to Riya. 'Karan, this is Riya. You remember her?'

Karan stared at her, looking puzzled, and Riya noticed with a little pang that his eyes were just like Dhruv's. 'I'm positive I've seen you before—only I can't think where.'

'Give up?' Chutki demanded, jumping up and down and then pronouncing triumphantly, 'She's the girl from the cupboard!' And as Karan's puzzlement deepened 'Dhruv *bhaiya's* cupboard, you dimwit.'

Sudden remembrance dawned on Karan's face. 'Oh, God, yes. You told me it was there! Dhruv gave me the thrashing of my life when I opened his cupboard to look for it.'

'Sorry,' Riya said, feeling immediately guilty.

Karan grinned. 'Don't be a nut. Chutki and I drove Dhruv crazy when we were kids. Where is he, by the way?'

'Dunno,' Chutki replied.

Karan sighed. 'So much for a happy family reunion. I understand the progenitors aren't here?'

Chutki shook her head, her normally merry little face sombre. 'Mum refused to come, and Dad didn't want to come alone. You haven't spoken to them yet?'

'Not yet. I guess I'll need to call them some time. I was hoping I'd meet them here. You getting along with them OK?'

'They're driving me crazy. It's so unfair—why am I stuck living at home while you boys get to globe-trot? If they don't let me leave this year, I'm going to run away to become a swimsuit model.'

'That's the latest, is it?' Karan asked. 'Good one. Though I liked the eloping with the milkman story the best.'

Riya stared at them, a bit bewildered at the sudden twist in the conversation.

Karan kindly explained. 'Chutki wants to become a fashion designer. Mum's OK with it, but Dad has other ideas.' He gave his sister an affectionate look. 'We've all had tussles with them about our careers. Dad wanted Dhruv to join the municipal planning division after he completed his architecture degree. And he wanted me to become an engineer when I wanted to be photographer. I must say Chutki manages them the best.'

'They want me to become a doctor,' she said with a sniff. 'I'm in my second year of medical college. But I also got a portfolio done.' She flipped open her phone and started scrolling through photos. 'Look at these. I've even got a modelling offer from a swimsuit brand. Mum nearly died of horror.' She snickered evilly. 'I've told them I'll go to med school, but if they don't let me do a fashion designing course in parallel I'll drop out and become a swimsuit model.'

'And the *doodhwala*?'

'The milkman's son fell in love with her, and madam told Dad she'd elope with him if he didn't stop yelling at her about her studies,' said Karan. 'So now poor Dad doesn't dare to even raise his voice to her.'

'And he also gets up at five-thirty to walk to the dairy and get the milk,' Chutki said happily.

Riya laughed till tears ran down her cheeks. 'So you boys don't help Chutki stand up for her rights, do you?'

Karan sobered a bit. 'Actually, Dhruv had the worst of it. It took him a long time to convince Dad to let him study architecture in the first place. And when I dropped out of engineering to take up photography things hit the roof—Dhruv took the brunt of it.'

'I don't remember much of that,' Chutki said, shrugging. 'Look—here's my milkman.' She scrolled to a picture of a shy-looking youth with large liquid eyes.

'Showing off our conquests, are we?' Both Riya and Chutki jumped as Dhruv spoke behind them. He was frowning slightly, and a wary look came into Chutki's eyes.

Karan clapped a hand on his shoulder, defusing the tension to some extent. 'Good to see you, *bhai*! Yes, Chutki was telling Riya about her milkman phase. Her latest is that she's going to try modelling if our errant parents don't shape up their ways.'

Dhruv's expression darkened again, and he shifted unconsciously, as if to block Karan and Chutki away from Riya. 'Do we need to discuss family matters in public?' he asked.

Chutki stared up at him, eyes widely innocent. 'Riya isn't "public"! She lived in our cupboard for *years,* remember?'

Dhruv laughed at that, though it came out sounding a little forced. 'So she did,' he said lightly. 'I'm not sure if she wants to hear the story of our lives right now, though.'

His gaze met Riya's and she started feeling a little more breathless than she should. *Control, control,* she thought, trying a few deep breathing exercises, and then blushing when she found Karan gazing at her curiously.

'Let's get back downstairs,' Chutki suggested, slipping her arm into Riya's. 'I promised Asha Bua we'd help her sort out the gifts for Madhu's family.'

CHAPTER FOUR

THE gift-sorting took time, and it was eight when Riya could finally slip into an empty room to change into the outfit she'd got for the wedding. She'd originally planned to wear a sari, but now more than ever she was glad that she'd given in to a mad impulse to buy the exquisite but very expensive *lehnga choli* that she'd found in a boutique near her office.

The sleeveless *choli* was tight-fitting, made of pale pink chiffon with a satin lining of the same colour, and very low-cut—the Wonderbra knock-off she'd bought on her last trip to Thailand gave her a respectable cleavage, and the colour perfectly complemented her skin tone. Her slim midriff was bare, and the *lehnga* was close-fitting around the hips, flaring out at mid-thigh to end with a swirl of material at her ankles. The entire outfit was covered in silver *zardozi* embroidery, the tiny hand-embroidered motifs picked out in painstaking detail. Lovely—but very expensive. And she'd probably get to wear it once or twice a year at the most.

She sighed, and then swiftly started doing up her face. She kept her make-up to a minimum, only emphasising her large eyes with kohl, and using a dash of lipstick on her lips. Her *dupatta* was a little wisp of chiffon that she draped loosely around her shoulders, before pulling her hair into a simple knot at the nape of her neck and securing it with a silver clasp. A few tendrils escaped and she let them be, giving herself a final critical look in the mirror before she rejoined the others.

Dhruv's breath caught for an instant as Riya came into the room—she looked so lovely that pretty much every other man, including his own brother, was staring at her. He caught Karan's eye. He grinned back at him unrepentantly—he'd figured out that his normally serious big brother had a thing for Gaurav's pretty flatmate, and had decided to get the maximum possible fun out of the situation.

The group of relatives and friends that made up the *baraat* finally left at nine, after an elaborate *sehra*-tying ceremony.

'Isn't he going to wear that ridiculous Bengali white cap thingie with pom-poms dangling near his ears?' Karan asked disappointedly. 'I was looking forward to seeing him in it.'

Riya shook her head. 'His mum put her foot down. The wedding is Bengali-style, but the *baraat* is going to be a Punjabi one, and the groom is going to be dressed like a Punjabi he-man—no pom-poms.'

'The circulation to his brain is getting cut off,' Karan said, gesturing towards Gaurav's flushed face under the heavy turban. 'The pom-poms may not be macho, but I think they're more practical. And he'd have looked *soooo cuuute*.'

Gaurav glared at him as Mrs Khanna hurried up to them.

'Boys, Gaurav's going to need help getting onto the horse.'

Karan's eyes widened. 'You're serious?' he asked

Dhruv. 'Gaurav-*baba* is going to ride through the streets of Kolkata on a white horse?'

'White mare,' Dhruv corrected him. 'Accompanied by a brass band. The *baraat* is the only Punjabi part of the wedding, and Aunty Asha wants to do it in style.'

It took the combined efforts of Dhruv and Karan to hoist Gaurav onto the horse, and he sat there sweating freely and looking totally helpless. 'The things one has to do for love...' he muttered.

'You look good, Gaurav,' Riya said soothingly.

And he actually did—the heavily embroidered *sherwani* concealed his bulk, and he looked a bit like a maharajah from olden times. The horse staggered a little under his weight, and started walking forward slowly.

Dhruv grabbed Riya's arm and pulled her into the centre of the *baraat* party. 'Get ready for some serious dancing,' he said, laughing down at her.

Riya cast a rueful look down at her high-heeled silver sandals.

'Take them off and give them to Karan,' he suggested, and Karan grabbed them eagerly—along with Chutki's voluminous bag and Dhruv's jacket.

'No dancing for me,' he said, hopping into the car that was carrying the gifts to the venue.

'Spoilsport!' Chutki yelled after him as the band struck up a tune and the party took off down the road.

It was only half a kilometre to the Hooghly River, and the wedding was to be on a floating hotel anchored at the riverbank. The *baraat* was boisterously noisy, dancing down the road to some of the latest Hindi film numbers. Dhruv and Riya had joined one of the younger groups, made up mostly of Gaurav's cousins and his CYB colleagues. The dancing was chaotic—

part-bhangra, part-Bollywood, and part plain, uncoordinated jumping around.

Riya walked alongside them for a while, careful not to get her toes trodden on, and then found herself whirled into Dhruv's arms. He was a good dancer, and Riya had to just follow his lead. Looking up into his laughing face, she had a sudden flashback to their college days, when he'd tried teaching her to jive.

They'd been at her house, and her parents and sister had been away, and they'd finally ended on the sofa in a tangled heap, kissing each other clumsily at first, and then more confidently as they got the hang of it. It had seemed so right—his hands at her waist, his lips on hers, and her arms locked tightly around his neck. But from the next day he'd turned cold, ignoring her in college and not taking her calls.

An involuntary shiver ran through her at the memory, and she moved unobtrusively away from Dhruv. He came to stand next to her, though, and they stood by the bank of the river to watch Madhulika's parents formally welcome Gaurav and his family into the hotel.

Gaurav looked nervous now, and Riya and Dhruv fell into step beside him as they walked up the gangplank and the stairs onto the open reception area where the wedding was being held. Madhulika was sitting on one of a pair of throne-like chairs, while everyone else was bustling around getting things ready. She wore a traditional red sari and a white *mukut,* with little dots of sandalwood paste along her eyebrows and forehead.

Her face lit up as someone yelled out in Bangla, *'Bor eshe gaeche!'* The groom is here! Gaurav beamed at her and hurried across the deck to take her hand, all traces of nervousness gone.

'They look so happy,' Chutki said, sounding uncharacteristically sentimental.

'Hope it lasts,' Dhruv muttered.

Chutki retorted sharply, 'It will. Gaurav-*bhaiya* is one of the nicest people I know, and Madhu's a darling. Right, Riya?'

'Right,' Riya said, smiling, but unknowingly Dhruv had added *Totally cynical* to the bullet points in the 'Cons' section of Riya's list. She had to firmly repress the urge to make a note right away, and she looked around for a distraction.

Happily, Karan was waiting for them.

'My feet are a mess,' Riya said as she took her sandals from him. 'And so is my hair.'

'Let's find a room where you can tidy up,' Dhruv suggested.

He took her down the stairs again, and they went into one of the hotel rooms that had been left open for guests to use. Dhruv shut the door behind them, latching it as it swung open again. He tossed his jacket onto the bed, and opened the bathroom door.

'The floor's wet, Riya,' he said. 'Don't come in. You'll ruin your *lehnga*.'

Riya stopped in her tracks. 'What do I do, then?' she asked. 'Stay here for the rest of the wedding?'

'No,' he said, putting his hands on her shoulders and sitting her down on the bed firmly.

Riya waited quietly as he fetched a small basin of water from the bathroom and set it down in front of her. He rolled up his sleeves, and, gently taking her feet in his hands, eased them into the water. Riya started to bend, but he pushed her hands away firmly. 'I've got this under control,' he said, 'Just hold your *lehnga* out of the way.'

'I didn't know you had a foot fetish,' Riya mumbled, but the feel of his strong hands caressing her feet was exquisite as he gently washed the dust off her feet. He took his time, running a little washcloth along the sensitive skin at the arch of her foot and stroking her ankles. His head was bent, and Riya couldn't stop herself from stretching a hand out and running her fingers through his hair.

He looked up then, smiling at her and turning his head to press a kiss into her palm. 'You've managed to cut your foot as well,' he said, standing up and going through the drawers in the bureau. 'There should be a first-aid kit somewhere here—let me get you a plaster.'

A door banged outside, and they could hear Mrs Khanna call out, 'Seema, hurry up—everyone's waiting.'

'Let them wait. We're from the boy's side,' they heard Aunty Seema reply, and Riya grimaced involuntarily. There was a pause, and then Seema said, '*Acchha,* Asha, who was that dark girl dancing with Dhruv?'

'She's Gaurav's friend,' Mrs Khanna replied. 'Dhruv knows her from college.'

Dhruv had gone very still, but at the last words he closed the drawer with a sharp shove and came back to kneel in front of Riya, gently taking her feet out of the water and drying them with a towel.

Aunty Seema's voice floated in again. 'Oh, OK. *Sundar hai,* but looks aren't everything. I hope Dhruv isn't getting carried away. I had two good Punjabi girls for him to meet—very well-to-do business families—and he calls me in the morning and says he doesn't want to meet them. It was so embarrassing; I didn't know what to do.'

Mrs Khanna made a soothing noise. '*Arre,* no, Asha.

All I'm worried about is that he shouldn't end up doing what his father did. Getting caught by a pretty face and regretting it for the rest of his life.'

Mrs Khanna's voice was suddenly sharp. 'He could do a lot worse than Riya. She's a lovely girl, well-educated and intelligent. What more do you want?'

'I always knew Asha Bua was a sensible woman,' Dhruv said, the smile back in his voice.

He finished drying her feet, and carefully inspected the tiny cut on the side of her foot before bending his head and kissing it gently. Riya sat very still as he put a plaster over the cut and gently slid her feet back into her sandals, buckling the thin silver strap around her ankles.

'All done,' he said, straightening up and carrying the basin back to the bathroom.

'Thanks, Dhruv,' Riya called out. She gave herself a minute before standing up—the kiss had turned her knees to jelly, and she didn't want to keel over and make a complete ass of herself. For the sake of something to do, she picked up Dhruv's designer jacket. 'You've messed up your clothes now,' she said, trying to shake the creases out.

He shrugged into the jacket. 'It doesn't matter,' he said. 'No one'll notice. It's not my wedding.'

'Why didn't you go and meet those girls your aunty lined up?' she asked later, when the two of them were alone during a lull in the ceremonies.

Dhruv said, 'I hadn't met you again when I agreed to see them. I told you—I wanted us to have some time together to get to know each other better.'

'What about the girls, then? Wouldn't they have expected…? Chutki told me one of them was supposed to be here tonight.'

'Chutki talks too much,' Dhruv said. 'Look, I don't see the purpose of this interrogation.'

His handsome face was furrowed. Riya shrugged. 'You're right. It's none of my business.'

'I didn't say that. Riya, if something is bothering you I'd prefer we discuss it in the open.' Her face must have showed something, and he said, 'I know I haven't been very open in the past, but—' *deep breath* '—that's something I'm trying to change about myself. So, anything you want to ask…' his dreamy smile flashed out '…now's the time.'

'OK,' Riya said, firmly battling down her immediate let's-jump-into-bed reaction to the smile. 'What's bothering me is that you agreed to an arranged marriage in the first place.' He looked puzzled, and she threw up her hands. 'It's archaic! Like a slave auction or something—going and looking at a dozen women and choosing one you think is up to your weight!'

'You're over-dramatising a perfectly civilised process—no one is being coerced into meeting me, and they have a choice, too. It's not like a girl I like is constrained to marry me. She has as much right to say no as I have.'

'As if they would,' Riya muttered.

'Two of them did, actually,' Dhruv said, and as Riya's eyes flew up to his in undisguised surprise he added, 'I'm not irresistible,' and then, 'though I quite like the idea that you think I am.'

Dhruv watched Riya's immediate descent into confusion with enjoyment. He hadn't been strictly accurate—one of the girls had confessed to having a previous attachment and the other didn't want to emigrate. Otherwise the girls his aunt had lined up had seemed surprisingly eager to jump into matrimony with him.

'Whatever,' Riya said, recovering quickly and returning to the attack. 'The point is, you don't seem to think *who* you marry is important, just that you get married.'

Dhruv sighed. 'I do think it's important. And I'm not dying to get married. But I'm thirty-two, and I'd like to have a family some day. The arranged marriage route seemed to make sense—both sides know what they're getting into, and expectations are set right at the beginning.'

Riya wrinkled her nose. 'Maybe I was wrong about it being like a slave auction. Sounds more like a business deal—like a merger or an acquisition. Select the lucky girl and draw up a little legal agreement: *The party of the first part, hereinafter referred to as the bride, unless repugnant to the context, hereby agrees to have sex twice a week with the party of the first part, while the party of the first part, also known as the husband, agrees to provide the bride with shopping money equal to or exceeding that hitherto provided to her by her paternal progenitor, otherwise known as her father, and adjusted for the prevailing rate of inflation as determined by the Reserve Bank of India.'*

She ran out of breath at the same time as Dhruv reached out and shook her. 'I've a good mind to spank you,' he said threateningly, but the corners of his mouth were twitching.

'Do you remember that guy Pappu who used to follow you around?' Dhruv asked. 'The one who was always peering at you through the library shelves while you shoved a whole hardbound set of *Advanced Thermodynamics* onto his foot?'

'Do I just! He scared the living daylights out of me when he followed me home that evening.'

'You didn't look scared,' Dhruv said, remembering seeing the slim girl from the library standing in the middle of the road, defiantly staring down the bunch of local goons surrounding her. He'd stopped his motorbike immediately—luckily Pappu knew him, and had backed off at once. They wouldn't have actually harmed her physically, but they could have made her life miserable for the rest of the college session. 'You were so hot-headed in those days,' he said musingly. 'I used to worry about you—the way you rushed head-first into everything.'

'Including relationships,' Riya said wryly.

Dhruv grimaced. 'At least you were sure of what you wanted. I admired you a lot for that. I was a confused idiot in those days. I thought I'd improved with age, but after meeting you again I'm not so sure.'

Riya's heart started beating painfully. 'You did say I could ask you what I wanted. *Why* were you so mixed up? I'm not asking for an explanation of what happened between us. I just want to understand what was happening with *you*.' The second the words left her mouth she wished she hadn't asked. He'd snubbed her pretty adroitly the last time she'd brought the topic up, and the odds were pretty high he'd snub her this time as well.

Dhruv looked into the distance for a few seconds without answering. He had been doing some serious thinking, and had finally come to the conclusion that he owed Riya at least a basic explanation, however difficult it was for him. 'A lot of things were happening,' he said finally, and then turned to smile at her. 'From what I gathered, Chutki and Karan haven't exactly been holding themselves back from discussing our parents?'

'I figured that they have issues with Chutki wanting to be a fashion designer,' Riya said cautiously.

'My dad does. And earlier he had issues with Karan being a photographer,' Dhruv said. 'But that's not the main problem.'

He hesitated again, and Riya half expected him to change the subject without any further explanation. He continued, though.

'They don't get along with each other. At all. They married for love—like I told you, my dad's parents completely freaked out, but they finally did agree to the marriage. My maternal grandparents refused to speak to my mother ever again. Even when my granddad was dying he didn't allow my mum near his deathbed.' His hands clenched on the railings. 'And for a while my parents were living in a joint family. Everyone ganged up against her—they made her life miserable. Dad was setting up his business, and used to be away all day, and my aunts and grandmother would drive my mum crazy. I think Aunty Asha is the only person who was ever nice to her. Finally, Mum managed to convince my dad to move out and live separately from the rest of the family. My grandmother never forgave her for that.'

'So what was she supposed to do? Stick it out with all those meanies?' Riya asked indignantly.

Dhruv shrugged. Riya's indignation was endearing, and of course she'd sympathise with his mum, seeing it from the female point of view. But he still wasn't sure if he was doing the right thing telling her all this. He hardly ever talked about his parents, even with his brother and sister, and strictly speaking none of this was relevant to the problems between himself and Riya. It was a relief telling her, though—it eased some of the tightness in his chest that came whenever he thought of his college days.

'From what I hear now from my aunts, my mum

didn't make an effort to adjust either. She made quite a big deal of being a Brahmin and vegetarian, and she used to cook her meals separately, and not let Karan and me eat food that had been cooked by anyone else. She used to speak to us in Marathi, too, which none of them understood.'

'I still think it was their fault,' Riya said.

'So did I—for many years. I'm not so sure now. Anyway, whoever's fault it was, my mum did go through a lot. And with Dad not being around much, it's not surprising that she began to wonder whether it was worth it. So they started having fights—Dad would expect her to attend family functions and she'd refuse, and they'd have these arguments which would get worse and worse...' His voice trailed away.

Riya said, 'Dhruv, you don't have to tell me if it's bothering you.'

'No, I think I *do* need to explain—in spite of what I told you in Mumbai. Even if it sounds like a bunch of lame excuses.' His voice had a bitter undertone. 'I used to envy you, you know. The few times I came over to your place your parents seemed to be such calm, well-adjusted people, and you and your sister would go running to them for every small thing that went wrong in your lives.'

'We still do,' Riya said with a smile in her voice. 'Mum's trying to break us out of the habit.'

Dhruv laughed. 'Without much success, I assume? So, like I was telling you, my parents had a really rotten relationship—I was thrilled when I finally left home for college. Then, around the time I met you, things got really bad. Do you remember I had to go home suddenly for a few days?'

'Yes,' Riya said. It was unlikely she'd forget—Dhruv

had changed so much after that visit. He'd always had a moody, dark streak to him, but after he'd come back it had become very pronounced.

'Well, that visit was because my father had found out that my mum was secretly encouraging Karan to take up photography as a career. She's always been the creative sort herself, and she thought he had real talent. They had a massive fight about it—Dad accused her of undermining his authority with us, and Mum said she was tired of him deciding how all of us should run our lives. Anyway, I don't think the cause of the fight was important. It was just that they hated each other by then—really hated each other—and finally Mum decided to leave him. She packed up her things, and Chutki's, and left. Karan was in the first year of engineering college, so he was already living in a hostel.'

'That's why you had to go home?'

Dhruv nodded. 'Mum didn't really have anywhere to go—she was staying at a friend's place, and I went to try and convince her to come home.' His face tightened in distaste. 'Dad didn't even bother to try and speak to her. I think Mum came back because she didn't have a choice. She couldn't stay with friends indefinitely, her parents wouldn't have her back, and Dad was threatening to stop paying Karan's college fees and mine. So she came home. But she didn't talk to Dad for two years after that. She used to cook his meals and look after the house, but she didn't speak a word. If she needed to tell him something she told Chutki, and Chutki went and told Dad.'

There was a pause. Riya didn't want to ask him more. She understood better why he had been the way he was in college. Marriages made in the previous generation were sacrosanct, and divorce was a dirty word. The issues between his parents would have torn him apart, and at the same time been too shameful to talk about. Funny how things changed with time. Chutki was only twelve years younger, but she had no compunction about speaking of her parents even to a comparative stranger. Though Chutki didn't reveal much, either, she thought, thinking of the bubbly little girl sandwiched between two silent parents. It was a wonder she'd emerged relatively unscathed from that kind of an upbringing.

Dhruv was apparently thinking the same thing. 'Chutki deals with the two of them so much better than Karan and I did. They started talking only because she flatly refused to carry any more messages. And she was only ten then. Even now she doesn't really want to leave home or become a fashion designer—she wouldn't have joined med school if she was serious about designing. It's more that she knows she has the upper hand over them if she's rebelling about something or the other.'

'Like saying she'll go off and become a swimsuit model,' Riya said, wondering if it was quite so simple. The whole conversation with Chutki earlier had sounded surreal—she didn't know anyone who had that kind of relationship with their parents.

'Yes, or marry the milkman's son.' Dhruv laughed wryly. 'I didn't know who to feel sorrier for—poor Yadav Chacha—or my parents. Yadav Chacha was so upset that his son had dared to even look at Drishti *bitiya*. But they've improved a lot—especially Dad, now that he knows that Mum can move in with either Karan or me if she really wants to leave. Anyway, I guess you get the picture now. Life was complicated, and I didn't want to get into a relationship at that stage. When I came back to college I thought I'd make sure we stayed just friends—but things got a bit out of control.'

'A bit,' Riya agreed, thinking back to that rainy afternoon in her parents' house. She'd done her best to hold onto him, probably realising subconsciously that if she let him go she'd lose him for ever.

He'd pulled away, though, finally standing up and saying in a hoarse voice, 'This isn't right. I need to leave,' and almost running out of the door. She'd had enough pride not to beg him to stay, but her heart had come close to breaking as she watched him go. She'd realised then that he didn't love her—and that realisation had hurt far more than the actual split when it came.

'I thought I was doing the best thing for both of us,' Dhruv was saying. 'I couldn't keep away from you, but I couldn't keep my hands off you, and I wasn't ready for any kind of commitment. In the end it seemed easier to just walk away, let you think whatever you wanted. You were a kid. I thought you'd forget about me soon enough.'

'I didn't,' Riya said, with a slight catch in her voice. 'I might have been a kid, but I really was in love with you.'

'Or you thought you were,' Dhruv said, and as she was about to reply he held up a hand, 'I know, I know. It's the same thing. It hurts just as much. It's just that I don't believe in love, Riya. Very few people are able to match up to the expectations the other person has, and it ends in disillusionment nine times out of ten. Or at least the intense "love at first sight" kind does.'

His brow furrowed as he thought about his parents. Love at first sight had turned to hate pretty quickly there. He wondered what Riya had expected from their relationship at seventeen. Commitment? A happily-ever-after ending? A surge of anger at her naivety then and now swamped him, and he looked away quickly. She was probably lucky he had ended things when he had, even if he'd done it clumsily—she'd have got really badly hurt if they'd gone further and he'd broken off with her at a later stage.

'What *are* you looking for from marriage, then, Dhruv?' Riya was asking quietly.

'Companionship. Mutual respect. Common interests. I'm not saying there shouldn't be physical attraction— a marriage wouldn't work without it—but it can't be the only thing.' His voice was steady, but a remnant of simmering anger made his words sound harsh and uncompromising.

Riya nodded, looking away for a second as her vision grew slightly blurry. Ever since she had met Dhruv she'd wanted to find out what lay behind his reserve, why he held everyone at arm's length. And ironically, now that he'd finally let down his defences, one of the first things she'd figured was that what he could offer a woman wasn't enough. When she decided to marry someone he had to be completely hers, body and soul. *And however much you'd like that someone to be Dhruv, it isn't gonna happen, girl,* she said to herself sternly. *It isn't even worth trying to take this any further.*

She looked up at him, making her smile artificially bright. 'I think the *pheras* are about to begin.'

Dhruv nodded. 'Let's get back.'

Gaurav and Madhulika had just started the first *phera,* circling the sacred fire as the priest chanted in Sanskrit. They had made a break from tradition here—instead of Madhu following Gaurav they were doing the *pheras* side-by-side, hand-in-hand, gazing into each other's eyes so intensely that the world seemed to shrink to contain just the two of them.

'If he doesn't look where they're going they'll get

barbecued,' Karan muttered, but even he looked impressed.

Riya watched, dutifully throwing handfuls of yellow rice whenever the priest's assistant prompted them to. *This* was what she deserved, she said fiercely to herself. Consolation prizes, however well-packaged, weren't enough.

CHAPTER FIVE

THERE were some more ceremonies after the *pheras,* but with the main part of the wedding over people started drifting towards the dinner buffet.

Riya paused to check her messages on her phone—there were two missed calls from her sister, and a text message: 'Call when you can.' Riya frowned. Her father had suffered a stroke a year ago that had left his left side paralysed for a while, and her immediate thought was that he might have been taken ill again. Physiotherapy had helped, but he still walked with a limp, and his overall health had deteriorated.

Troubles of the heart temporarily forgotten, Riya walked to a secluded corner to try and call her sister, Shreya, back.

Dhruv found her fifteen minutes later, seated at a table and chewing her lip worriedly. Her sister's call had been to say that the recent rains had badly damaged their parents' home, part of the ceiling and one of the walls having collapsed. They were both OK, but the house needed immediate repairs which would cost around five hundred thousand at the minimum. Shreya would have helped them, but she'd just invested almost all her free capital in the dental clinic she was setting up with her husband. Besides, now that she was married her parents refused to take money from her, saying that a wife's earnings belonged to her husband. They had been broad-minded enough to give their daughters a good education, but of late had turned alarmingly traditional on things like this.

Five hundred thousand… Riya's job was reasonably well-paid, but five *lakhs* would be difficult to raise without selling off almost all her investments. A lot of her savings had already gone towards her dad's hospital bills—he had never invested in medical insurance, and her company policy only covered her, not her parents. Added to which she'd bought the new car a few months ago, and splurging on things like designer *lehnga cholis* didn't help. Evidently an austerity regime was called for.

Riya bit back a sigh. Money had always been short in her family—she didn't grudge a rupee she'd spent on her parents, but at times she wished she wasn't the only one with a head for money.

'Doesn't it make more sense for them to sell the house and buy a smaller place that's easier to manage?' Dhruv asked impatiently, once Riya had explained what had happened.

Riya shook her head. 'The house belonged to my grandparents—my dad grew up there. So did my sister and I. I don't think any of us wants to sell it.'

Something in her expression warned Dhruv not to push the discussion further. Evidently Riya had her demons, too. He wanted to reach out and pull her to him, wipe that worried, care-ridden look off her face, but he didn't think she'd let her guard down with him enough. He'd need to give her a lot more time before she started trusting him fully.

'If you need help, let me know,' he said abruptly. 'Money or otherwise.'

Riya flushed darkly, only the part about money registering. She'd always been sensitive about her family being badly off, and she'd regretted telling Dhruv about the house almost the second the words were out of her mouth. She'd rather be boiled alive in smelly mustard oil than play beggar maid to Dhruv's or any other man's King Cophetua.

'I'll manage,' she said tersely and looked up at Dhruv. 'I'm really tired. D'you think it's OK if I leave now?' Dhruv hesitated, and she said quickly, 'You don't need to come with me—I'll send the car back for you. I need to pack and get to bed early. I'm leaving on the seven-thirty flight tomorrow morning.'

Mentioning money had been a bad idea, Dhruv realised a little too late, remembering how touchy she'd been in college about financial favours, insisting on paying her share even for a cup of coffee.

'If you're sure? I wouldn't mind leaving with you, but I need to hang around for a while and do the polite thing with relatives. Haven't met some of them in years.'

'Yes, of course. See you around, then.'

She was gone before Dhruv could say anything more. He frowned, wishing he could have gone with her, but he did need to spend some time with his relatives— he'd been talking to Riya through most of the wedding, completely ignoring the other guests. And he'd see her again in Mumbai soon enough.

Riya's sister called her back when she was in the car.

'Hope you aren't panicking, kid,' she said worriedly. 'I shouldn't have called you, only I thought you'd want to know. Dad's OK, and so's Mum. They're moving in with me and Vivek till the house gets fixed.'

'That's a relief,' Riya said, and it was. Her dad, while

he was the sweetest man alive, could be alarmingly stubborn about some things. She'd been worried that he'd insist on staying on in the damaged house rather than 'impose' on his older daughter—there was an old tradition that said a man should never accept food and drink in his son-in-law's house, and Riya's father was quite capable of trotting that out as an excuse to stay on in his own home.

'Aryan's thrilled,' Shreya continued. Aryan was Shreya's three-year-old son who adored his grandparents. 'I wish Mum and Dad would move in here permanently. It'd be a relief to know someone was around while I'm at work.'

'Don't think that's going to happen, sis. You know how Dad is.'

'I know.' She sighed, and then perked up. 'Hey, you'd said you met that guy from your college, Dhruv. I did a Google search on him and checked out some of his pictures. He doesn't have a social networking page, but there are articles about him on lots of news sites. Some new project he's working on. He's hot, by the way. Good teeth, too.'

Riya said indignantly 'Do you think of anything other than teeth? And why are you doing Google searched on him anyway?'

'I'm a *dentist*!' Shreya said defensively. ''I can't help noticing teeth. And I was trying to find out more about him because I think you have something going on with him that you're not telling me about. Be careful, though—you can't trust a man with light eyes.'

Riya felt her ears going a little red. She wasn't sure she wanted to discuss Dhruv with her protective older sister. They'd always been close but Shreya, married and a mother, was no longer the friend she'd spent so many nights giggling over boys with.

'Dreaming about your hottie?' Shreya asked teasingly when she didn't reply. 'By the way, you might want to tell Mum about him. She's been getting very worried about you.'

'Worried about me? Why?'

'Because you don't seem to want to marry and settle down,' Shreya said. 'She's very proud of how well you're doing, but you know Mum—she doesn't think a woman can be happy without a man in her life and at least a couple of kids. And you refuse to even consider an arranged marriage. So if things are getting serious with Dhruv you should probably let her know.'

Riya grimaced. 'I don't think things with Dhruv will ever be serious,' she said. 'We're looking for very different things from life.'

Only she wasn't sure any more *what* she was looking for, she thought as she let herself into her flat the next morning. Gaurav's stuff was still lying around, but the flat felt very empty. She slumped down onto the sofa, trying to identify the weird mood she found herself in. *I'm lonely,* she realised, and laughed suddenly. She'd never lived alone in her life before—till she'd finished college she had lived with her parents, and then had moved to a hostel while she did her MBA. Ever since she'd started working Gaurav and she had shared a flat. Now, however, she was senior enough to be eligible for a flat of her own. Her firm hadn't reallocated Gaurav's room to anyone, assuming she'd want to continue there alone.

Her phone rang while she was still figuring out how to deal with the unexpected emotion. A completely different kind of feeling swamped her when she saw the display on the phone.

'Hi, Dhruv,' she said.

'Hey, Riya. Things OK at home?'

Riya shut her eyes for a second. She was as susceptible to the voice as she was to the man—and admittedly he had a very nice voice. Deep, with a slight gravelly undertone, and the slightest accent that he'd acquired in his years overseas. She could imagine him leaning forward in his chair, his golden eyes concerned.

'Riya?'

'Yes, things are better, thanks,' she said hastily. 'My parents have moved into my sister's house temporarily, and they're trying to find someone who can fix the house.'

'Is everything all right, then? You sound a little upset.'

'I'm fine. Just got back—I think it's sunk in only now that Gaurav's moved out.' She laughed a little shakily. 'I'm so used to having someone around to nag.'

'Missing him?' Dhruv asked gently.

'Yes,' Riya said, and was horrified to find that tears were running down her face. She scrubbed at her cheeks angrily, thankful that Dhruv couldn't see her.

'Would it help if I took you out for dinner?' he asked. 'I'm back in Mumbai this afternoon, and I don't have any plans for the evening.'

'I have some office work to catch up on,' Riya said quickly. The temptation to see him again was almost irresistible, but she couldn't trust herself enough to let him into her life again.

'It's several hours till dinner time,' he said. 'I'm sure you can get it done by then. I don't like the thought of you sitting around and moping all alone.'

Great—that made her sound like some kind of a basket case. Probably she should just stop babbling and tell him outright that she'd decided she didn't want to see him again. If he asked why, she could tell him that it was because she had decided to enter into a period of abstinence and self-denial for religious reasons, and having dinner with hot men was one of things she'd sworn to give up. Highly unlikely he'd believe her, but at least he'd write her off as a head case and avoid her in the future.

'I don't really feel like eating out,' she hedged, after the silence grew a little uncomfortable. 'And there's work tomorrow, so I need to get to bed early...'

'I get the message,' he said drily. 'OK, I won't force you into having dinner with me. But I do need to drop by some time today to pick up some stuff I left with Gaurav.'

'Where is it?' Riya asked suspiciously. This was the first she'd heard of him leaving any of his belongings with her flatmate. Then, of course, it wasn't likely that Gaurav had remembered, either, much less bothered to tell her.

'It's a small grey suitcase,' Dhruv said. 'It has my passport and some other papers—it didn't make sense carrying it to Kolkata and bringing it back, so I left it there. I'm not sure where Gaurav's put it.'

'Think I saw it somewhere,' Riya admitted grudgingly. 'I'm home all day. Pick it up whenever you want.'

'Good,' he said, and she pictured him smiling that slow, delicious, smile of his into the phone. 'I'll come across at around eight. That OK?'

'Yes,' Riya said, and then, realising that if he was coming over anyway refusing to have dinner with him was pointless, and just a little rude, she said, 'Listen, if you're coming over at eight, do you want to have a quick dinner at home? I'll ask Ranjana to cook something.'

'If you're sure?' Dhruv said. He could tell Riya was struggling with something, even though he didn't know the reason, and he didn't want to push her too hard. 'I don't want to intrude if you want to be alone—I can order in room service or something once I'm back at the hotel.'

Guilt swamped her, and she said hurriedly, 'No, it's nothing like that. It's just that after all those late nights during the wedding I don't feel up to going out again.' Her body was already thrumming with excitement at the thought of seeing Dhruv again, and it was definitely up to far more than just going out for dinner. Time for extreme self-control again, she thought, biting back a sigh.

Her rambling thoughts were pulled back in line by Dhruv's crisp voice.

'Right, I'll see you at eight, then—if that's not too early?'

'Eight is good,' Riya managed, and she closed the call quickly before she said anything stupid.

Riya spent the rest of the day getting the flat in order. She put the stuff Gaurav had left lying around back into his cupboard, for him to pick up when he returned to Mumbai. Then she cleared out the bathroom, scrubbing the tiles till they shone and throwing out the half-used toiletries lying around.

Gaurav had been a wonderful flatmate, but he'd been messy—like many men, he appeared to think tidiness would detract from his masculinity. The living room was littered with old newspapers and magazines, and junk mail was piled high on the dining table. Riya heaped up the papers in the kitchen for the wastepaper man to collect the next day, and went through the mail to make sure she wasn't trashing anything important. The clearing up was cathartic in a way, helping her deal better with the thought of living alone for the next few months, perhaps the next few years.

She left the kitchen alone—that was Ranjana's domain—restricting herself to ordering some groceries over the phone from a nearby store. Ranjana arrived at six, full of questions about 'Gaurav-*saab*'s' wedding. Riya showed her a few photographs, and she oohed and aahed over the bride's outfit.

'Gaurav-*saab* looks good, too,' she said. 'Like a *rajah*. No photos of you?'

Riya clicked her phone shut. 'No,' she said. 'Ranjana, can you make dinner for two people today, please? Make chicken biryani, if you can, and that special raita.'

'Who's coming over?' Ranjana asked.

'A friend of mine,' Riya said repressively. Ranjana was a great gossip, and she didn't want her telling everyone in the building that Gaurav-*saab*'s cousin was visiting her, even though Gaurav-*saab* was away.

Riya took her time showering and washing her hair. She decided to dress simply, slipping into a pair of jeans and a sleeveless tunic-style *kurti*. The *kurti* was raw silk with *kantha* embroidery—casual, yet chic. She slipped a few antique silver bangles onto her wrists, and was towelling her hair dry when Dhruv rang the bell. She put the towel down, and clipped her hair back before she took a deep breath and went to open the door.

Dhruv stood there, looking almost sinfully gorgeous. He wore a black full-sleeve shirt and dark jeans, and the fine material of the shirt stretched across his broad shoulders to clearly reveal the strength of the muscular body underneath.

'Good evening,' he said, smiling slowly at her, and then, as she kept looking at him without moving out of the doorway, 'Can I come in?'

Riya stepped back to let him into the flat, more flustered than she cared to admit even to herself. Her heart was racing, and she was finding it difficult to think straight. He was carrying a bottle of wine, which he put on a side table.

'The flat looks different,' he said, looking around.

It did. Riya had changed the curtains to a set she'd bought a long while ago but hadn't put up because Gaurav thought they were too 'girly'. There were vases on the side tables, holding dried flower arrangements that she'd run out in the afternoon to buy. She'd also moved a lamp and some of the bright cushions from her room to the living room, and put up an old framed piece of Rajasthani embroidery on the wall. There were tea-lights in little holders on the dining table but she hadn't lit them, thinking a candlelit dinner would be too suggestive—bright fluorescent light was safer.

For a few seconds after Dhruv's comment she wished she'd left the room alone. He'd seen it just before they left for Kolkata, and she didn't want him to think that she'd gone to all that trouble to impress him. His next words allayed her fears though.

'This is a definite improvement,' he said, gesturing at the room. 'Earlier it had a bit of an unwashed Bohemian bachelor pad look to it. I assume that was because of Gaurav?'

'Yes, well, he didn't like me "prettifying" the flat too much,' Riya said, recovering some of her composure. 'He said he needed a certain amount of mess to feel comfortable.'

'And you're missing him all the same?' Dhruv raised his eyebrows in mock horror, and she laughed.

'Terrible, isn't it?' she said. 'I must be a glutton for self-punishment. But he used to sulk so much whenever I tried to tidy the flat or change anything that I gave up. What'll you have to drink, Dhruv?'

Dhruv smiled a little wickedly. 'You don't need to play the hostess with me, Riya. We're a little past that stage, don't you think?' She blushed, and he relented, saying, 'Just water for now, please.'

He couldn't resist teasing her—for a while he'd been taken in by her carefully assumed self-composure, but now that he'd figured out just how much his presence affected her it was amusing to knock her off her plate now and then. His own reactions to her were just as powerful, but he was far more experienced than she was, and able to cloak them better.

His phone rang, and he looked down at the display, frowning. 'I'm sorry, I'll need to take this call—my bank's been messing up, and I need to sort a few things out.'

Riya went into the kitchen to fetch the water. Dhruv had stepped out onto the balcony to take the call, but little snippets of his side of the conversation drifted back to her. 'Trading account', and 'tax benefits', and 'three *crore* investment portfolio'. Her heart gave an uneasy little thump. Three *crores* worth of investments? Three hundred million rupees? That was a lot of money by any standards, and from what she could hear it was only a small part of his net worth.

Little things began to fall into place. Her colleague Rishabh's excitement when he heard that Dhruv was a partner in Icarus Designs—Aunty Seema's insistence that only a rich bride would do for Dhruv. She'd assumed he'd done well—he dressed well, and had the automatic air of command that most successful people possessed—but she hadn't realised that he was *rich*. Not just well-off, but indecently, stinking rich.

From a middle-class, not-very-well-off family herself, Riya had always been inordinately careful to steer clear of men with money, and Dhruv's money seemed like yet another insurmountable barrier between the two of them.

She went back into the room once Dhruv had finished his call, and silently handed him a glass of water. He took it and, setting it down on a table next to him, stretched a hand out to draw her down on the sofa next to him.

'Why're you so nervous?' he asked gently. 'I don't bite.'

She shook her head. 'It's been a peculiar day,' she said. 'Maybe we shouldn't have met up today.'

Her voice shook a little, and Dhruv said nothing but leaned over, and started gently massaging the back of her neck.

Riya's felt her bones turn to mush as his fingers moved down her spine. 'Dhruv, don't,' she said finally, her voice coming out more shaky than she wanted it to.

He didn't stop, though. He moved his hand from her back to her hair, gently releasing the clip that secured it at the back of her head. Riya said nothing, sitting very still as he twisted a lock of still-damp hair around his fingers.

'I've missed you,' he said softly, and Riya turned to look at him, willing herself to hold his gaze.

The familiar out-of-control sensation was about to

overtake her when he moved his hand to the back of her head and pulled her closer. Certain he was about to kiss, her, and equally certain that she wouldn't be able to control things if they went any further, Riya jumped to her feet.

'Let's eat,' she said hastily.

Dhruv nodded. He'd decided to take things slowly with Riya, but as usual he hadn't been able to keep his hands off her. *Damn,* he needed to be able to handle things better. This was the first time he'd felt so out-of-control in a relationship, and he didn't like the feeling. Perhaps continuing to see Riya wasn't such a good idea after all. Her reactions were puzzling. She seemed to be pulling back at every step, as if she was scared of being with him. The Riya he'd known before had been fearless, clear about what she wanted, and not afraid to speak her mind.

'Dinner's served,' Riya called out, and Dhruv joined her at the dining table.

Their conversation was stilted for the first few minutes, until a chance remark made Riya laugh. Dhruv watched her, admiring the slender column of her throat as she threw her head back to laugh. A piece of a half-forgotten Urdu song that he had heard many, many years ago came to mind, and he repeated the lines softly.

'"*Tum itna jo muskura rahe ho. Kya gham hai jisko chhupa rahe ho.*" You've been smiling so often, what is the hidden sorrow behind the smile?'

Riya leaned back in her chair, no longer laughing but looking at him, an odd smile playing about her lips.

'So some things about you are still Indian, are they?' she asked.

Dhruv raised his eyebrows. 'Most things about me

are Indian,' he said. 'I haven't been out of the country for very long.'

Riya shook her head. 'Not really, Dhruv. Your accent has changed, you only speak English now, and your mannerisms are different.'

Dhruv frowned. Some of his relatives had made similar remarks during Gaurav's wedding, but while he had found them irritating he had ignored them. Riya's tone was faintly disapproving, and that bothered him, though he didn't stop to analyse why.

'I'm as Indian as I ever was,' he said. 'My accent might have changed without me realising it. Now that I'll be spending a lot more time in India I expect I'll start sounding *desi* again.'

Riya shrugged. 'I doubt it,' she said, getting up to fetch a bottle of mango pickle from the refrigerator. She hadn't meant to go down this path—she had a prejudice against people who emigrated—and Dhruv didn't really display any of the more obnoxious NRI traits. His not speaking Hindi any more *had* been bothering her, however. In college they had always spoken to each other in a mixture of Hindi and English, and Dhruv's English-only conversation struck an alien note now.

To change the topic, she asked, 'How's your plan to set up a Mumbai office going? Or is it too early to ask?'

'I'd done a lot of the groundwork before I came here,' Dhruv said. 'This city is a mess, though. Things take a long time to move, and the infrastructure is in terrible shape—I'm beginning to regret the decision to set up an office here.'

Riya flared up immediately in defence of her beloved city.

'People like you who leave haven't any right to

comment,' she shot at him. 'You've hardly given it two weeks before starting to chastise.'

Dhruv groaned mentally. He wasn't in the frame of mind to go into the reasons for his leaving India, and his reasons for coming back. He'd left partly because of his career, but mainly because he'd wanted to get the hell away from his family. He'd come back for a whole different set of reasons—and Riya's re-entrance into his life had turned them topsy-turvy. The more he saw of her, though, the surer he was that his decision on how long he'd stay in India depended on how things panned out with her.

'I think I have every right to comment,' he replied after a brief pause. 'I left because the opportunities here were limited. And, while I'm very willing to give the city a chance, the amount of corruption there is in the system isn't heartening.'

'If it's so bad, why bother to come back?' Riya asked, all set to do battle. 'Why not stay on in nice, clean Singapore? Or, better still, go live in the US or the UK, or maybe Armenia, or the Czech Republic. And I believe Kazakhstan is quite nice as well. Why India?'

'I'm coming back because I want to live in my own country. For a while at least.' He paused. 'If you don't mind, let's change the topic. It's a little too heavy to make good dinner-time conversation. Seen any good movies lately?'

Feeling very firmly put in her place, Riya tried to recover her poise, failed, and then making a little face, muttered, '*Movie toh abhi zindagi mein chal rahi hai.* There is a movie playing in my life right now.' Dhruv's habit of controlling a conversation, deciding what he wanted to talk about and what he didn't, was infuriating and difficult to fight.

Dhruv laughed and, getting up from his chair, came across the table to take her chin between his thumb and forefinger and tilt her face up towards his. 'Very *filmi*. All you need is a camera,' he said mock-approvingly. 'I'm sorry I cut you off. I'm just not feeling like a serious conversation right now. And I know what you're like when you get on your soap-box. Completely carried away, you get.'

'Talking like Master Yoda, you are,' Riya said crossly, as he released her chin and patted her cheek lightly.

The pat was almost brotherly, but it still made her senses tingle. She made another face as he went back to his chair. Her good resolutions about keeping her distance from him were beginning to melt as rapidly as an ice cube in the Thar desert.

'Are you done?' she asked finally, noticing his empty plate. 'Dessert? Or would you prefer coffee?'

'Coffee, please,' Dhruv said, getting up to help her clear away the plates.

'There's only instant,' Riya said, rummaging about in the kitchen cupboards. 'Damn, Ranjana seems to have hidden the sugar. It's a miracle the coffee's actually in the right tin—'

'Without sugar is fine,' Dhruv interrupted, as Riya put the water on to boil.

'Oh, that's good, then,' Riya said. 'I don't take sugar, either, and in any case I can't find it.' She turned and gave Dhruv a little push. 'Wait in the living room. You're making me nervous. I'll probably poison the coffee by mistake if you keep hanging around here.'

The bit about him making her nervous had slipped out by mistake—it was totally unfair how her normally sharp brain turned to mush at a speed inversely proportional to the physical distance between them. She turned to take the water off the hob, and gave a stifled little yelp as her hand touched hot metal. She held it under the tap for a few seconds, and then finished making the coffee, managing to pour it into two cups and carry it out without any further accidents.

Dhruv put aside the magazine he was leafing through when she came into the room. 'Who subscribes to this?' he asked, pointing to the little stack of *National Geographic* that had remained in the magazine stand after she had cleared out all of Gaurav's junk.

'I do,' she said, and then, at his surprised look, 'What? I look more the gossip magazine type?'

'More the business magazine type, I would have thought,' he countered. 'You seem very serious about your job.'

Riya shrugged. 'Not outside office hours,' she said, handing him his cup of coffee, and then stilling suddenly as he put it down and took her hand in his to examine the angry red burn mark on her thumb.

'How did you manage this?' he asked.

'Hot vessel,' she said, shrugging and feeling a bit like a snake under the aegis of a particularly skilled snake charmer as she tried to will herself to take her hand out of his warm clasp.

He raised her hand gently, and before she could make out what he was about to do he put his lips to the mark. Her thumb found its way into his mouth without her having any say in the matter, and the thought of resisting didn't even cross her mind when he finally released her hand to take her into his arms. He kissed her slowly and thoroughly, and she was trembling when he drew away after several minutes.

Clumsily, she stood up and stumbled back a few

steps. 'We shouldn't be doing this,' she said, almost in a whisper.

'We'd be mad not to,' he said, and came closer to her, not touching her, but looking deep into her eyes with a challenge she found impossible to resist.

Her heart beat hard at her own boldness as she slipped her arms around Dhruv, standing on tiptoes to press her lips against his. The response was instantaneous, his arms coming around her, pressing her close to his hard body, his mouth hot and insistent on hers.

All coherent thought flew out of her head and they only just about made it to her bedroom, collapsing on the bed in a tangle of heated limbs. All she was conscious of was the feel of his lips on her skin, the delicious weight of his body on hers, and the sound of his voice whispering her name over and over again. It was as if they could never have enough of each other—until sheer exhaustion claimed them and they fell asleep, still tightly wrapped in each other's arms.

Eight hours later, Riya's eyes flew open. It was morning—she could make that much out—though very early. The patch of sky she could see outside the window was still a dull, steely grey. She turned to look at Dhruv, sleeping silently next to her, one arm still curved possessively around her waist. Her lips curved as she remembered last night. She stroked a hand gently over Dhruv's hair, and he muttered something in his sleep as he pulled her closer, the hand on her waist moving up to find her breast. For a second, she was tempted to snuggle back up to him, and wake him very, very slowly, but then, with a sigh, she slipped out from under his arm.

She was carefully folding up the jeans she had worn the night before when she became conscious of two golden eyes watching her carefully. 'Good morning,' she said softly, turning to look at six foot two of half-awake and totally gorgeous male stretched out on her bed. She was rewarded by a slow smile, and her heart gave a little stutter at the thought of waking up like this every morning for the rest of her life.

In your dreams, she told herself cynically. *There's no way he'd stick with you.* She'd been stupid, thinking she could manage to be alone with Dhruv without them ending up in bed together—she could resist him about as easily as her three-year-old nephew could resist a tub of chocolate-chip ice cream. And she'd be even more stupid to think that she'd be able to manage a light-hearted, purely physical relationship with him without her heart getting involved.

There was no way he'd even consider marriage with her now—if he'd come to India looking for a bride he'd want one with all the traditional virtues, and virginity was usually the first requirement. Even if he was willing to overlook the fact that she'd slept with him, there was also the undeniable fact that she hadn't been a virgin at the time. She'd heard enough from friends who'd 'gone a bit too far' with a boyfriend and then had him turn around and accuse them of being loose. Dhruv was far too sophisticated to make an accusation of that sort, but she would bet anything that he'd stopped thinking of her as serious marriage material. Assuming he'd ever thought of her that way in the first place.

The only sensible route open to her was to treat this as a one-off—both of them had lost control, but no harm done; they were mature adults and could move on with their lives. That would give him an exit option, and she had no doubt that he would take it. Her hands clenched. At no point during the night had he said that he loved her, or even that he cared, and she'd be a fool to expect him to say it now.

Dhruv was sitting up in bed, and the sight of his tanned golden torso was making it even more difficult for her to think.

'What time is it?' he asked. He was still not fully awake, but he wanted Riya back in bed with him. His body was already begging for a repeat of the previous night.

'Almost seven,' she replied, coming to sit next to him in response to his outstretched hand. 'I need to head out now—I have to be in the office by nine.'

He pulled her close, burying his face in her hair, not wanting to let her go. Ever. 'You can take the day off,' he suggested.

Riya shook her head mutely against him. This felt so right, but it was so, so wrong. The night had been a colossal mistake, and she was already tempted to compound it further by breaking every one of her carefully thought out early-morning resolutions.

So what if he breaks your heart? the evil little imp in her head prompted. *What are you going to do with it anyway? Put it in a glass case to admire when you're fifty? Why not enjoy whatever time with him you have, and let the future take care of itself?*

Because she was already half in love with him, she thought despairingly. She couldn't trust him not to hurt her, and already the thought of letting him go was almost unbearable. She had to do it before she got in any deeper, before he lost whatever respect he still had for her.

'I have a mountain of work to catch up on,' she said finally, her voice muffled against his broad chest.

'Smallish mountain?' he asked, his breath ruffling her hair. 'Sub-Himalayan?'

She shook her head, laughing slightly while her breath caught in her chest.

'More like a K2 or a Kanchenjunga,' she said, and, as he showed no signs of releasing his hold, 'Let me go, Dhruv. I really do need to get into the office, and *you* need to leave before Ranjana lands up.'

Dhruv frowned as he let her get up. The night had been incredible, Riya eager and willing, and while he'd not really thought about what would happen afterwards, the last thing he had expected was her calmly packing up to go to work in the morning.

'Why do I need to leave before Ranjana arrives?' he asked, picking up his crumpled jeans from the floor and sliding his long legs into them.

Riya almost threw something at him. 'So that she doesn't realise you spent the night here, of course,' she said, trying to keep her voice calm 'She'd be scandalised out of her wits if she knew.'

Now that Dhruv wasn't touching her any more she was able to think more clearly, and other ramifications of the previous night were beginning to occur to her. Nothing mattered as much as the basic fact that she'd slept with him when he didn't really care about her, but the thought of having other people know about it too made it almost intolerable.

Dhruv turned slowly to look at her, his eyes opening wide in astonishment.

'Why does her opinion matter? This is none of her business—she's the cook, for God's sake!'

'That's so easy for you to say,' Riya said derisively. 'I *live* here, in case you hadn't realised. It's tough enough being a single woman living alone, without the entire world knowing that you've been sleeping around. Not that I'd expect you to understand.'

'Now, what does that mean?' Dhruv swung her around to face him. He was finding it difficult to keep up with her mood swings. She had moved from being apparently indifferent to being upset in a matter of seconds, and he had no idea why.

'Why does it matter anyway?' Riya said. 'You've got what you wanted. Why hang around any longer?' Her tone was challenging, and she knew she was behaving like an idiot. If Dhruv had had the slightest intention of sticking with her, she was driving him away with every word.

'This is crazy,' Dhruv muttered under his breath.

Riya felt her heart twist a little. She turned away to hide her expression, but not soon enough.

His annoyance melted as he saw how truly lost she looked, and he pulled her against him to kiss her forehead, trying to ignore the way he hardened as soon as her body came into contact with his. 'What's wrong, sweetheart?' he asked, his voice gentle. 'I know this went a bit a faster than you wanted, but we can sort things out.'

Riya didn't answer, though she let him hold her for a while. Her body was still rigid as she fought off the tears that threatened to turn her into a little pool of helpless need at his feet. Finally, when she'd managed to muster some self-control, she stepped away from him, her face still averted.

'I'm sorry,' she said, her voice coming out a little gruff. 'I guess I'm not used to this. You can leave when you want. Though I'd prefer it if Ranjana didn't see you.' She picked up a set of work clothes from the top of her bureau. 'I need to go and get ready,' she said. 'I'll be late for work.'

She was looking right at Dhruv now, clearly expecting a response from him, but he didn't know what to say. He could see that Riya was still shaken up, and he didn't want to risk upsetting her further. And, whether he admitted it or not, he was fairly shaken up himself. There had been something incredibly moving about the way Riya had given herself to him the night before. He'd never before felt the same sense of total oneness with a woman, and having Riya turn on him the next morning was unexpected, to say the least.

Every fibre of him ached to pull her back into bed and resolve any doubts she had there, but he could see that he needed to give her some space. Extreme self-control, he thought wryly, remembering what she'd said to him on the phone before she left for Kolkata. Though in his case he'd need several cold showers before he could even start thinking about self-control.

He kissed her quickly and stepped back to pick up his shirt from the floor. 'I'll shower in Gaurav's old bathroom,' he said, turning to give her a quick smile, 'so that I'm out of here before Ranjana arrives. I'll call you later in the day.'

Riya nodded and closed the bedroom door behind him. He still hadn't said anything that suggested any kind of future together for the two of them, and Riya's heart ached so much she felt it would split in two. Thankfully she'd not made the colossal mistake of sleeping with him assuming that he'd want to marry her, or even suggest a long-term relationship. All she had to do now was make sure that she never saw him again if she could help it.

She stayed in the bedroom till she heard the front

door close behind Dhruv. Her composure sagged for a minute, tears springing to her eyes, but she dashed them away angrily and, squaring her shoulders, started getting ready to leave for work.

CHAPTER SIX

OVER a week later, Riya pulled up in the parking lot in front of her office, handing the attendant her car keys and a ten-rupee note. 'Park it inside whenever someone vacates a slot, OK?'

The attendant grinned at her as he slid behind the wheel. He'd probably keep the engine running for a while, so that he could relax with the air-conditioning on, but it was small price to pay in exchange for a decent parking slot at nine-fifteen a.m.

Riya ran into the building—even though it was a week since she had returned from Kolkata she was still behind with work. A meeting with a new client was scheduled for nine forty-five, and she had all of ten minutes to go through the brief.

She found it difficult to concentrate, though, with memories of her night with Dhruv crowding through her head. She hadn't seen him since the night in her flat, though he'd called a few times. He'd been out of town for a couple of days on site visits, and after he returned she'd avoided meeting him, pleading work as an excuse. She'd not even spoken to him on the phone for more than a few minutes each time, saying that she had meetings to go to, or people visiting.

Maybe that hadn't been such a good idea after all, if

it made her feel so lousy. Maybe she was being stupid, trying to force his emotions and hers into a cookie-cutter model of the perfect relationship and throwing the whole thing away when it didn't fit. What if it wasn't meant to be perfect? What if she was jettisoning something real and very precious in exchange for a mirage? And, she thought, her mouth turning down a little at the corners, the sex had been *so* good.

Now, with all her evasions, she'd made sure that Dhruv would never come near her again. All emotional tangles aside, that would be devastating. She'd probably end her days in a nunnery, or something, after she'd spent the next ten years of her life searching for the perfect man. And maybe get sacked before that—she'd been staring at the documents in front of her for fifteen minutes without taking in a word. She started again at the beginning with a sigh.

The brief was straightforward enough, but halfway through the client meeting it came out that she was expected to spend three months in Hong Kong working on the project.

'But, Sudarshan,' she protested to her boss in an undertone after they'd wrapped up, 'I have two other projects running. I can't just drop them.'

'This is more important,' he hissed back, his eyes almost bugging out of his head as they did whenever he was agitated. 'There's no way we can afford to lose this client. What's the matter anyway? I thought you liked travelling?'

She shrugged. It was true that one of the attractions of the job when she'd first taken it up had been the travel, but that had palled very soon. 'I'm not crazy about it,' she said—though the more she thought about it, the more appealing the prospect of three months out of the country seemed. At least it would take her out of the immediate range of temptation that being in the same city as Dhruv exposed her to every day.

'You women,' Sudarshan said unkindly. 'It's always something or the other. Next thing you'll be getting married, and then you'll want to work nine-to-five, and then you'll go on maternity leave...'

'No, I won't,' Riya snapped back, incensed. 'Don't be unreasonable, Soody. I'll go.' She marched out of the room without a backward glance.

Looking at her phone, she saw that she had a missed call from Dhruv. She couldn't postpone talking to him indefinitely. Logic said that it would be best to make a clean break, tell him that their night together had been a mistake and that she wasn't in the market for a short-term fling. He hadn't mentioned anything about wanting a more permanent relationship—to be fair, she hadn't given him a chance to—but she didn't have much hope. The temptation to take whatever he was offering was immense, and she'd been putting off speaking to him in the fear that she'd agree to something that would only end up breaking her heart in the long run.

Finally, with the determined air of an early freedom-fighter being marched off to jail by the British, she picked up her phone and dialled his number. It kept ringing, and she was about to put the phone down with a sigh of relief when he answered.

'Sorry, I was in the gym,' he said.

An image of Dhruv, all sweaty and delicious, imme-diately sprang to mind, and she tried to push it out of her head. This was the problem with her, she thought—no self-control. She could deal either with straightforward lust, or with the kind of emotional rollercoaster she'd been going through the last few days. Both together were difficult to handle.

'No meetings today?' she asked.

'Some,' he said.

There was a long pause. So long that Riya began to wonder if he'd hung up on her. When he finally spoke again, his voice sounded more friendly, as if he'd thought things over and decided to try a different approach.

'Do you want to come over to the hotel for dinner tonight?'

Riya thought it over. It was such a tempting thought— dinner could lead only to one thing, and if they were in his hotel she didn't need to bother about people finding out. But her rational side, for once in the ascendant, promptly put forward a dozen reasons against meeting him, and she sighed in defeat.

'I don't think it's a good idea, Dhruv.' Her colleagues in the next cubicle were looking at her curiously—there must have been something in her voice that betrayed that this wasn't a normal conversation. Riya got up and walked in to an empty meeting room. 'Maybe we should just give things a rest.'

'Why?' he asked baldly, and she was thrown into immediate confusion.

'Everything moved a bit too fast last time,' she said. 'If we meet again, we might…we might…'

Dhruv listened grimly to her voice trail off before he spoke. 'We might have sex again. Is that it?' he asked, his voice hard. 'And, from the way you've been avoiding me, I assume that would be a terrible thing?'

'I didn't mean—' Riya started to say, but he cut in.

'So, no sex,' he said. 'If you want, I'll put it in writing. Send you an e-mail. Would that be enough for you to agree to meet me? Take a few minutes out to tell me exactly what the hell went wrong?'

The irony of the last few words struck him as soon as they were out of his mouth. For the last few days he'd been going through something very similar to what he imagined Riya had been through when he'd walked out on her twelve years ago. He might even have been tempted to believe that her behaviour after their one night together was calculated to pay him back—only Riya was not the kind of person who would do something like that. She might storm and rave and break things, or even go silent, but there wasn't a mean or vindictive bone in her body. This wasn't about payback—the thought of seeing him again was making her run scared.

For the first time in his life Dhruv Malhotra found himself pursuing a reluctant woman. A sharp and completely uncharacteristic streak of possessiveness had flared up in him after the night in her flat—the feeling that she was *his,* and had been since the day he'd first kissed her, no matter what had happened in the intervening years. There was something archaic about that feeling—something more basic than the soppy emotion popularised in women's magazines and Bollywood movies—and he was damned if he'd let her get away with the weak excuses she'd been fobbing him off with.

'I need some space,' Riya was saying huskily, and he found himself almost groaning out loud in frustration.

The sound of her voice was bringing back every passion-filled moment they'd shared, and the thought of staying away from her any longer was rapidly becoming unbearable.

'How long?' he asked. 'Are you OK with meeting

later this week? I'm in Nagpur next week, visiting my parents.'

'Yes, later this week sounds good,' Riya said, and then realised that if her Hong Kong visa came through she'd probably be out of the country by Thursday. Which would be a blessing, all things considered, giving her the time she needed to sort out and deal with her feelings for Dhruv.

She put the phone down and took a deep breath, heading towards Rishabh's desk. There was something else she needed to take care of before she started obsessing about her love-life.

'You got the paperwork done?' she asked, leaning across the partition between his cubicle and the next.

'I did—but are you sure, Riya?' Rishabh asked, his usually pleasant face a little worried. 'I mean, it's a fabulous deal as far as I am concerned, but I don't understand why you're selling your car six months after you bought it.'

'Let's just say I don't like driving any more,' Riya said. 'You want it or not?'

'Of course I want it!'

Rishabh was a reasonably good friend, in spite of their rivalry at work, but he was also not the sort to pass up on a good deal. He slid the cheque he'd been filling out across the table, and Riya took it quickly. She'd bought the car cash down, thankfully, so there was no loan to pay off—Rishabh's cheque would go into her bank account, and she'd transfer the money to her mother's account the next day.

'Take care of my baby, OK?' Riya said as she signed the papers to transfer the car registration to Rishabh. She took the red frog charm off her keyring and tossed the keys across to Rishabh. 'The other set of keys are with the car park attendant,' she said. 'I didn't get a parking slot in the morning.'

Rishabh nodded and left his cubicle, taking the papers with him.

Riya passed a hand over her face. For a few seconds she had felt very close to tears—she'd saved up for two years to buy the car, and it had meant a lot to her—then she straightened her shoulders and marched out of the room, straight to the ATM in the building to deposit the cheque. At least she'd still see the car once in a while, she consoled herself, and then laughed at her own stupidity. She was happy she had sold the car to someone she knew rather than to a used-car dealer—this way she felt a little less guilty about abandoning her red darling.

The rest of the day was crazily busy, meeting following meeting, so that Riya hardly had time to breathe let alone have lunch. She managed to grab a sandwich in the canteen around four o'clock, and was halfway through it when Sudarshan sent her a message saying he wanted the proposal for the Hong Kong project typed up and on his desk by the end of the day. Riya groaned, abandoning the sandwich and going back to her desk. The proposal would take a good five hours.

Rishabh was holding a *bhajiya* party in his cubicle to celebrate his 'new' car—he had the grace to look a little embarrassed when Riya showed up.

Her work area was too noisy to concentrate in, and she went into an empty meeting room to work on the proposal. Her thoughts kept wandering, though, back to Dhruv. Several times she almost picked up the phone and called him to say that she *would* have dinner with him, but she stopped herself. Images from the night they had spent together danced across her brain, and she found herself reading and re-reading the same documents without being able to make any sense of them at all.

She finally managed to complete the first draft of the proposal at around eight. When she went to collect the printout from the printer she saw that the office was almost empty. Her boss's cabin was empty as well, and his secretary was in the process of packing up for the day.

'Melissa, I thought Sudarshan wanted this before he left?' Riya asked.

Melissa, a motherly woman in her late fifties, turned around, looking harried.

'Why are you still here, Riya?' she demanded. 'Didn't you read the e-mail we sent out? The rains have been really bad today, and the admin team asked us to send people home.'

'Flooding?' Riya asked, her heart sinking as she remembered the last round of floods. 'I didn't get the e-mail. I was working on a proposal, so I unplugged from the LAN. Soody said—'

'Mail it to him and go home—he left two hours ago,' Melissa interrupted crossly, adding something under her breath that sounded suspiciously like 'the selfish bastard'.

She took the printouts from Riya's hand and went in to Sudarshan's cabin to put them on the desk.

'The trains have stopped running, and the roads are very bad. You drive home, don't you?'

Riya nodded, not wanting to explain that she no longer had a car.

'You can come home with me,' Melissa offered. 'My son's coming over to pick me up—I'm in Colaba, so we'll be home in ten minutes.'

'Thanks, Melissa, but I think I'll try getting back to my flat,' Riya said. She'd been to Melissa's place a couple of times—her two sons, daughter-in-law and baby grandson all stayed with her, in a tiny two-room flat, and fitting in an extra person would mean one of them having to sleep on the enclosed balcony.

'If you're sure?' Melissa said. 'It's no trouble. Dinner's already made, too, and there'll be more than enough for all of us. Cheryl's made chicken vindaloo. Let me know if you change your mind. You're always welcome.'

An hour later, Riya was wishing she'd taken up Melissa's offer. It was pouring so hard she could barely see across the road, and she'd been standing outside the office for twenty minutes, vainly trying to get a cab.

'You'll have to swim, then,' one cabbie said when she told him she wanted to go to Parel. 'It's as bad as the twenty-sixth of July rains in 2005.'

Another told her cheerfully that he was planning to switch off his lights and go sleep in the cab. Most of the yellow-tops didn't even stop, whizzing past her cheerfully, and the call-cab numbers were all engaged. There weren't too many people around, and even the shops and restaurants down the road were pulling down their shutters.

After ten minutes more Riya gave up and trudged back into office. In the 2005 floods it had taken her almost twenty-three hours to get home, and she'd had to wade through waist-deep muddy water for most of the way—she was not keen on repeating the experience.

The burly security guard salaamed as she went back in. The office was completely deserted now, but she felt safe with Gaikwad at the front desk—he was an old friend, and had escorted her from police station to police station when she'd had to file an FIR for a stolen laptop. Back in her work area, she surveyed the scene. Her cubicle was definitely not big enough to lie down in, even if she was OK with stretching out on the floor. There was a couch in Sudarshan's room, though, and she headed there, carrying the little box of energy bars she kept in her desk for emergency rations.

More than ever now, she wished she had accepted Dhruv's invitation for dinner—a five-course meal followed by mind-blowing sex was a better option to eating sticky two-month old energy bars and sleeping alone on an undersized and extremely slippery couch any day.

One of the gods above must have been tuned into the right channel, because her desk phone rang at exactly that instant. Riya ran back to answer it, saying, 'CYB—Riya Kumar speaking,'

'What *exactly* are you still doing in the office?' demanded Dhruv's completely unexpected and impossibly sexy voice.

'How'd you get my office number?' Riya asked stupidly.

He made a dismissive sound. 'It's not exactly a state secret. Your mobile's unreachable, by the way. I've been trying it for the last hour.'

'Must be the rains,' Riya said, and there was a pause.

She wasn't sure why Dhruv had called, but she didn't know how to ask him without sounding impossibly rude.

On the other end of the line Dhruv was barely holding on to his temper. He'd been out at meetings the whole day, and had got back to his hotel early once he'd figured that the situation in the city was worsening. Since then he'd been trying to call Riya to make sure she was OK, and hadn't been able to get through either on her mobile number or on her home number.

He'd finally called enquiries for her office number, and someone had transferred the call to her desk.

'Are you driving home?' He'd checked the news, and the roads to Parel were badly waterlogged. She'd have made it if she'd left for home an hour ago, but it was unlikely she'd get more than halfway there now. The obvious solution was for her to come over to his hotel—it was only a kilometre from her office, and South Mumbai never got flooded. Given the way things were between them, he didn't want to suggest it—though he did want to be sure she had somewhere to go to.

'No,' said Riya. 'I don't have my car today.' *Or tomorrow,* she thought, *or the day after.*

'Shouldn't you have left early, then? Unless you were planning to sleep in office?' He'd meant the last bit sarcastically, but after the guilty silence that followed he said incredulously, 'Is that what you were going to do?'

'Um…' said Riya, trying to buy some time. She was normally good at telling over-protective men exactly where they got off, but the skill didn't extend to Dhruv.

'Riya,' Dhruv said threateningly, and she hastily rushed into speech.

'I am, actually. I had to work late, and I didn't realise it was raining, so I thought it made more sense just to stay here.'

'I assume your office has windows?' Dhruv asked, more sarcastic than ever. 'Did it occur to you actually to look out of one at any point during the day?'

'And has it occurred to *you* that you sound like a cranky old man?' Riya retorted spiritedly. Arguing on random topics she could handle—even with Dhruv. 'Some people have to work for their living, you know. I don't have time to laze around, looking out of windows and waiting for my prince to charge up on a white horse and rescue me from the nasty wet.'

Now she'd asked for it, Dhruv thought. 'I'd suggest you find a window, then, and start looking out of it. Because, space or no space, I'm coming there to collect you in exactly fifteen minutes.'

He smiled grimly at the sudden yelp of alarm that came from the phone. Served her right for telling him earlier in the day that she needed 'space', and now babbling on about princes and white horses. He liked women to be self-sufficient, but Riya carried independence to almost maniacal levels.

Riya recovered quickly. 'You won't be able to get here,' she said smugly. 'There isn't a taxi to be had, and you'll have let your car go by now.'

'Oh, I'll be there. Don't worry,' Dhruv retorted. 'Pack up your stuff and wait—and see if you can get your phone to start working.'

Her phone, Riya figured, was not working for the simple reason that it had run out of charge. She plugged it in, and sat herself down to wait on Sudarshan's faux-leather sofa, whiling away the time reading a book on organisational leadership that she'd found on his desk. The words kept getting jumbled in her head, and she finally put the book down in exasperation.

A floor-to-ceiling window made up one side of the room and she went to look out of it, the way Dhruv had suggested earlier. The rain was lashing down in sheets, and occasional flashes of lightning lit up the sky. Paradoxically, the wildness of the weather had a calming effect on her, giving her the feeling that something bigger and more powerful had taken control over her life. The decision on whether or not she should meet

Dhruv before she left for Hong Kong had been taken out of her hands by the rain.

She leaned her head against the cold glass of the window, watching the trees in the park opposite sway in the wind, and let her thoughts drift—almost jumping out of her skin when the phone rang loudly a few minutes later.

'There's a *saab* here, waiting for you,' Gaikwad said cautiously when she answered. 'Says his name is Dhruv Malhotra.'

Riya felt her heart begin to pound unevenly, and she had to stop in the middle of the room and take a few deep breaths. So much for the rain calming her down, she thought distractedly. If Dhruv kept turning up in her life, at this rate she'd need to get a pacemaker installed before her next birthday.

When she went out, however, she felt a lot better. For once, Newton's Law of every action having an equal and opposite reaction seemed to be working between her and Dhruv. He was stalking around the reception area like a caged panther, and his eyes positively smouldered when he saw Riya. She stared at him for a bit, completely mesmerised by the sheer animal beauty of the man. He was soaked through, his shirt plastered to his body, and his hair was curling damply around his temples.

'You're wet,' she said finally, stupidly.

'It's raining,' he said impatiently. 'I thought we'd finally established that fact.' But his eyes gentled as they rested on her, and Riya started feeling a little less gauche and schoolgirlish.

Gaikwad cleared his throat. Evidently he wasn't comfortable with little Riya-madam going off with this tall, menacing, rain-sodden stranger—Dhruv's hotness was not likely to find favour with the huge security guard.

'It's OK, Gaikwad—' Riya started to say, but Dhruv interrupted her, saying a few quick sentences to the man in Marathi. Gaikwad melted immediately, beaming almost paternally at the two of them.

'What did you say to him?' Riya demanded hotly as they got into the lift.

Dhruv shrugged. 'Nothing important.'

'I heard you say *jiddi,*' Riya said. 'I don't speak Marathi, but I bet that means stubborn—same as in Hindi. Were you talking about me?'

'Relax, princess,' Dhruv said. 'The whole world isn't talking about you all the time.'

This was so patently unfair that Riya stared at him, speechless for a few seconds, by which time the lift doors had opened and they were out on the pavement.

Riya fumbled for her umbrella, looking up when Dhruv said, 'I don't think that's going to be much use.'

The fact that he'd been carrying a helmet finally clicked in her head, and she said, 'Oh, my God, where did you get the motorbike from?'

'Borrowed it from the guy at the hotel reception,' Dhruv said, holding out the helmet. 'Wear this. There's only one.'

The motorcycle was lethal-looking—a black souped-up Yamaha with a skull and crossbones sticker on the fuel tank. Riya gingerly perched herself side-saddle behind Dhruv, holding the helmet in her hand. She was used to bikes—Dhruv had had one in college, too—but it was ten years since she'd last sat on one.

'Sit astride and wear the helmet,' he ordered over his shoulder.

'I'm wearing a skirt, in case you hadn't noticed,'

Riya said. 'I don't want to go through town displaying my panties to the general populace. And helmets aren't compulsory for the pillion-rider in Mumbai. *You* wear it.'

Dhruv's expression as he looked over his shoulder suggested that she'd have to pay for the panties remark later. He didn't say anything, however, kick-starting the bike and taking the helmet from her to hang it from the handlebars.

The rain pelted at them as Dhruv took to the main road. Even though she was partially shielded by Dhruv's body, each raindrop stung. Also, sitting side-saddle while trying to hold on to her bag and a large plastic packet was a slippery business. The plastic packet carried the spare set of clothes she kept in the office, and things kept threatening to slide out.

Dhruv stopped at a signal, and she quickly looped the handle of her handbag around one wrist, tucked the packet under her arm, and slid the other arm around Dhruv's waist to hold herself securely against him. She felt his body tense up, but again he didn't say anything—though he drove faster than before.

They reached his hotel in ten minutes, and Riya slid off the pillion to stand shivering under the awning while Dhruv spoke to the guard at the security check booth at the entrance. The man recognised him, taking the bike from Dhruv and waving the two of them through. Riya felt acutely conscious of her wet clothes and lack of luggage, but the hotel staff were too well-trained even to blink an eyelid.

Dhruv's room was small but luxurious—this hotel was more like a set of service apartments than a regular hotel, but it was five-star deluxe, and from what Riya had heard the room rates were exorbitant. Yet again the niggling thought struck Riya that Dhruv was way out of her league financially.

She was still standing awkwardly in the middle of the room, worried that her streaming clothes would stain the expensive upholstery, when Dhruv came back into the room after dropping the bike keys at Reception.

Dhruv frowned. 'You need a hot bath if you don't want to die of cold,' he said, going into the bathroom to get a couple of towels. He tossed one to her and, stripping off his shirt without the least bit of self-consciousness, threw it onto the floor. 'I think there's a bathrobe in the cupboard—use that for now, and we'll figure out what to do about clothes for you in the morning.'

'I have clothes,' Riya said primly, pointing towards the plastic bag. 'I keep a spare set of clothes in the office during the monsoons. And I'll be getting back home tomorrow anyway.'

Dhruv said nothing, but kept looking at her in a way that made her toes tingle. She was acutely conscious of her wet blouse clinging lovingly to her breasts, and as his eyes drifted towards them, she blushed bright red and said, stumbling over the words, 'Can I use the bathroom first, then? I'm freezing...'

'Sure,' he said, and started walking towards her.

Riya stayed rooted to the ground, so nervous she couldn't speak. He was opposite her now, his bare chest just inches away. The temptation to touch him was irresistible, and she put her hand on his chest, right over his heart. The steady beat calmed her, and she looked up into his eyes, a little shy but able to hold his gaze steadily. He touched her hair lightly, brushing the damp tendrils away from her face, and, leaning forward, kissed her very gently on the lips. She kissed him back, tentatively at first, and then more confidently, teasing him gently with her tongue. They were both breathless when they broke apart a few minutes later.

'You need to get out of these wet clothes,' Dhruv said huskily, his hands going to the buttons of her blouse.

Riya stepped back hastily, suddenly self-conscious. Their first night together had been tempestuous, and she'd hardly noticed where her clothes had gone in her eagerness to feel his bare skin against hers—today, however, in the full glare of the fluorescent light, she felt embarrassed, and a lot less confident about her body than she had before.

Dhruv seemed to understand, putting his hands on her shoulders and giving her a slight push towards the bathroom door. 'Go and take a shower,' he said, and as she opened the bathroom door to go in he called teasingly after her, 'Call me if you need any help.'

Once inside, Riya surveyed her flushed face in the mirror. Her half-dried hair curled wantonly around her face, and her cheeks were flushed. The white shirt was still clinging damply to her body, and the fragile lace of her bra showed very clearly through. 'You look like a tart, my girl,' she muttered to her reflection, and turned away to strip off her clothes and get under the shower.

Ten minutes later, face scrubbed and hair neatly dried and combed back, she emerged from the bathroom swathed in the huge white hotel robe.

Dhruv looked up from the bed as she entered the room. He was still shirtless, but he had exchanged his rain-soaked jeans for a pair of tracksuit bottoms, and was reading the latest issue of *Newsweek*. The room was darker now, lit by only the reading lamp next to the bed and a small lamp over the dining area.

'There's a washing machine in the kitchenette,' he said. 'In case you want to put your clothes in.'

She nodded. Her clothes were a mess, and her watch had been ruined by the water, with moisture accumulating over the dial. It was an inexpensive one, and she slid it off her wrist and threw it into the trashcan before going off to find the washing machine.

Dhruv looked after her, a slight smile playing around his lips. He found her sudden awkwardness endearing—while he didn't expect every unmarried woman to be a virgin, there was still enough traditional Indian male left in him to value innocence over experience.

Riya finally managed to get the washing machine started—it was a front-loading model, and she wasn't used to the controls.

Dhruv watched her quietly. The instinct to drag her into bed as soon as she finished was strong, but after the last time he wanted to take things slowly.

'What do you want to have for dinner?' he asked, hoping his voice didn't betray the sheer lust that had him in its grip. 'There are a couple of good restaurants in the hotel, and a coffee shop, or I can order something in from outside.'

Once he mentioned food, Riya realised she was starving—only she hated the thought of going downstairs and sitting down for a formal dinner.

'Don't you have any groceries here?' she asked, opening a few cupboard doors and then giving an excited squeal as she located some packs of instant noodles. 'Can we have noodles? Please?' she asked, giving him such a comically beseeching look that he laughed.

'Of course,' he said teasing her gently. 'I should have known—I offer you a *cordon bleu* meal, and you want to have instant noodles. Figures.'

Riya made a face at him and took a pan out of another cupboard. She filled it with water, measuring the correct amount carefully. Dhruv came up behind her, putting his arms around her and gently nuzzling the nape of her neck.

'You're a minx—did you know that?' he whispered into her ear and, unable to resist temptation any longer, turned her around to kiss her.

She responded instantly, going on tiptoe to reach his mouth better, and sliding her hands up his hair-roughened chest.

They sprang apart a few minutes later when they heard the gentle hiss of the water boiling. Riya pushed her hair off her face and quickly retied her robe, which had come undone.

'Dinner first?' she asked Dhruv, looking up at him mischievously.

He nodded, watching her as she broke the noodles up and added them to the boiling water, along with the flavouring. He was finding it difficult to gauge his reactions to her—at present he was finding it difficult even to think straight with her soft, warm body so close to his.

To distract himself, he went across to the mini-refrigerator and dug out a little package of cheese, slicing it up to put on the noodles. 'We used to eat this stuff all the time in the hostel,' he said.

Riya came up to peer over his shoulder. 'Gourmet cheese?' she asked. 'You had refined tastes in college, I must say.'

'I think I had pretty good taste in college,' he said, his eyes roaming over her in a way that made her blush. 'But what I meant was instant noodles with cheese on top.'

They ate slowly, laughing slightly at the ridiculous

parody of a candlelit dinner. In its way, however, the dinner was probably the most romantic one she'd ever had, Riya thought as she watched Dhruv put the dishes in the sink half an hour later. At that moment she was closer to being in love with him than she ever had been before.

Done with the dishes, Dhruv turned around, his golden eyes gleaming cat-like in the poorly lit room. 'Time for dessert?' he asked, and held out his arms for Riya.

She stood up, and crossed the room to him.

CHAPTER SEVEN

RIYA woke the next morning to the sound of her mobile phone ringing.

Dhruv groaned and opened his eyes. 'Switch the damn thing off,' he growled, pulling her back into bed.

Riya managed to grab at the phone before she landed on top of him.

'Hi, Sonali,' she said, sounding a little breathless as she answered the phone. Dhruv had woken up thoroughly, and now had her pinned against the head board.

'Riya, where *are* you?' Her next door neighbour sounded worried. 'I tried calling you several times last night.'

'I, um, stayed over with a friend,' Riya managed, looking down at the top of Dhruv's head as he began to nuzzle at her left breast. *Some friend,* she thought, trying to push him away before she started moaning into the phone and lost whatever shreds of reputation she still possessed.

'Oh, OK.' Sonali sounded relieved. 'Somewhere near office, then?'

'Yes,' Riya said distractedly. Dhruv had managed to uncover both her breasts and was inspecting them closely, as if wondering which to favour with his attention first.

'You should probably stay there for a few more days,' Sonali was saying.

This caught Riya's attention, and she sat up quickly. 'Why, Sonali? Isn't the building OK?'

'The meter room got flooded again,' Sonali said. 'We haven't had any power since last night, and the lifts aren't working. The water's going to run out soon. too—the pumps won't work without electricity.'

Riya digested this, running her fingers through Dhruv's hair. He'd stopped what he was doing to listen.

'Stay on,' he mouthed at her, and she nodded lovingly, bending her head to give him a light kiss.

'How are you guys going to manage, Sonali?' she asked. Her neighbour had two small children, and she didn't see how they could stay on in a building without electricity and water.

'We're moving to a friend's place nearby,' Sonali said. 'Everyone's moving out except for that crazy couple on the second floor. I'll let you know when things are OK. Till then it's best that you stay over at your friend's place. Maybe you could come over and pick up your things, but you'll need to climb twenty floors to get to your flat.'

'Looks like you're stuck with me for a few days,' Riya said, looking at Dhruv.

'My pleasure,' he said throatily, lifting one of her hands to his lips.

She slid down the bed a little to kiss him. 'When are you off to meet your parents?'

'It was supposed to be this weekend,' he said, 'but I'll shift my flight to next weekend instead.'

'No, don't,' she said, kissing him again. 'I can move to a friend's place, and my flat should be usable in a few days.'

Dhruv said nothing, but he was surprised to find that he hated the thought of her leaving. Usually he had a mental time-limit for a relationship—six months at the outside—and he had never, ever asked a woman to move in with him. Two nights with Riya, however, had him aching to keep her by his side for ever. The sensible part of his brain still warned against rushing things with her, but he was finding the thought of a permanent commitment easier and easier.

Not wanting to explore this line of thought any further, he pulled Riya into his arms, covering her mouth with his.

Riya got into the office late—it was almost ten when she walked in. The office was half-empty, though, and the few people who had made it into work were standing around the water cooler, swapping stories about how bad the floods had been. Her boss, Sudarshan, was the only one working—he had returned the client proposal she'd left on his desk the night before, and he even had the grace to look a little guilty about going home without telling her.

Riya avoided the group near the cooler, not wanting to explain where she'd been the night before. Several of her colleagues stayed in the same building as her and were likely to ask questions.

It couldn't be helped, she thought as she booted up her laptop. If the rains hadn't been so bad she probably would have been able to avoid meeting Dhruv before she left for Hong Kong—as it was, the decision had been taken out of her hands, and she was back in some kind of relationship with him. She was still unsure about his feelings for her, or even if he had any, but she'd never felt so alive in her life. It was almost worth the heartbreak that was sure to come, she thought. All she needed to do was keep her head and get out of the relationship before he figured out how much she cared for him.

There didn't seem much point going back to her flat until the electricity was restored—she didn't relish the thought of climbing up twenty flights of stairs to retrieve her clothes and toiletries. So she spent her lunch hour shopping in Fab India and Westside, buying three sets of sensible, value-for-money *churidaar kameez* to wear to work till her flat was accessible, and some not-quite-so-sensible lingerie. The lingerie cost a lot more than the clothes, and Riya stared at the final bill in dismay. Her new austerity regime seemed to be going awry yet again.

To compensate, she skimped on lunch, picking up a *vada-pav* from a roadside stall on the way back to the office.

In spite of her preoccupation with Dhruv, she managed to get a fair bit of work done, completing the revisions to the client proposal Sudarshan had asked for, and mailing the final document to the client. She even managed to go and visit McQueen in the parking lot. Rishabh had parked the little red car facing outwards rather than inwards, the way she normally did, and somehow that irritated her intensely.

Dhruv picked her up after work—in a chauffeur-driven car this time. She made a face as she got into it. 'I liked the bike better.'

He pulled her close and kissed her thoroughly. 'We can't do this on the bike,' he said. 'Do you like the car better now?'

Riya cast an agonised look at the driver. 'Dhruv, don't,' she whispered, blushing a vivid crimson.

Dhruv released her and laughed. 'You're cute when you're embarrassed—d'you know that?' he said.

She mock-punched him on the arm. 'That's not the kind of cute women aspire to,' she said. 'Where are we going for dinner?'

Dhruv had chosen a fairly exclusive little restaurant in Colaba. The clientele was varied—right from elderly Parsi couples to Page 3 celebrities who looked barely out of their teens—but what everyone had in common was that they looked rich. Riya looked down at her clothes in dismay. She was still wearing the spare clothes she'd carried with her from the office the night before—a *salwar kameez* set that was a couple of years out of fashion—and she felt completely out of place.

'Couldn't we have gone some place less fancy?' she whispered to Dhruv as the snooty head waiter sailed off to find them a table.

Dhruv's brow furrowed. 'This doesn't look particularly fancy to me,' he said. 'But if you don't like it we can find something else.'

'No, this is OK,' Riya said hastily.

But it wasn't. She went to enough posh restaurants on client lunches and dinners, but she didn't really enjoy them, preferring the several inexpensive but quaint little eating joints that dotted Colaba and the Fort area. Not wanting to fuss, however, she followed Dhruv into the restaurant, thankful that the table they were given was in a secluded little corner, screened from the rest of the room by a large bank of potted palms. Evidently the restaurant wanted her hidden away as well; she must be seriously reducing their cool quotient.

She cast a discreet look around to see if there was anyone she recognised in the room. A striking woman in her early forties looked vaguely familiar, and Riya thought she'd seen her on TV, holding forth on a recent government scam.

Dhruv was pushing a little gift bag across the table. 'I got something for you,' he said.

Riya took it from him. The gift bag had a beautifully wrapped little square box inside, which opened to reveal a watch in delicate tones of silver and gold. It was lovely, but Riya looked up, suddenly uncomfortable.

'Why, Dhruv?'

He shrugged, not wanting to make a big deal about it, though he'd spent over an hour choosing the gift. 'I saw you throw away your watch last night, so I thought I'd get you a new one.'

Riya smiled uncertainly, barely restraining herself from saying, *But this is expensive.* She wasn't sure herself what was bothering her—the gesture of buying her a watch was unexceptionable, but the watch he'd chosen cost far more than any watch she had owned before. Looking at it, she thought it was probably more expensive than all the watches she and her entire family owned put together.

'If you don't like it I can exchange it for another design,' Dhruv said, misinterpreting the reason for her lack of enthusiasm. 'I picked this one up because the picture of the model wearing it reminded me a little of you.'

Somehow the last sentence made it all OK. Riya looked up and smiled at him. 'I love it. Thank you!' she said.

'Are you sure? You were eyeing it as if it was a particularly repulsive species of spider.'

Riya laughed, taking the watch out and sliding it onto her slim wrist. 'I was a little taken aback, that's all,' she said. 'I expected chocolates or something of that sort—

my ex-fiancé used to shower me with them, and I never did manage to convince him that I don't like sweets.'

Dhruv laughed, but his eyes had turned a little watchful at the mention of her fiancé. Her remark in Kolkata about 'technically' not being a virgin had bothered him more than he liked to admit even to himself, but he hadn't wanted to ask questions when he didn't have a right to the answers.

'What was he like?' he asked carefully after a few minutes, and then, as she gave him a blank look, 'Your ex?'

Riya laughed. 'Nice,' she said. 'He was really, really nice. Way too nice for me.' She was still smiling, as if she'd remembered something amusing.

'Are you still in touch with him?'

'Oh, yes,' she said. 'It was his daughter's birthday last month—I got her a finger painting kit and he was furious. She ruined all the walls in his flat.'

'He's married?' Dhruv asked, unable to keep the surprise out of his voice.

'Yes,' Riya said, grinning. 'When we split up he told me that he'd never be able to look at another woman, and would probably die a bachelor. Then he met this really cute girl at work, and got engaged in two months.'

'On the rebound?' Dhruv suggested, finding it difficult to believe that anyone could have forgotten Riya so quickly.

Riya frowned. 'No, I don't think so. He and I weren't really suited, and Suchita is perfect for him. Their baby is adorable, too.'

Riya's phone beeped, and she fished it out of her bag, grimacing as she saw the text message. 'Sorry. I'll have to reply to this,' she said. 'Minor crisis at work.'

Dhruv nodded, watching her as she keyed in several lines of text.

'Bad day?' he asked when she was done.

Riya sighed. 'Busy. I thought I'd end up missing dinner with you, but then thankfully my boss was ordered home by his wife and I could leave.'

'Your boss seems something of a tyrant,' Dhruv said. 'By the way, I have a dinner meeting tomorrow. Remind me to ask the hotel for a spare keycard for you tonight.'

'I mightn't be there tomorrow night,' Riya said thoughtlessly. 'I spoke to my neighbour just before I left work and she said there's a chance the electricity will get restored tomorrow morning.'

Dhruv's hand stilled for a second in the act of carrying a spoon to his lips. Somehow he'd assumed that Riya would stay with him for as long as he was in Mumbai— he'd booked his room for a month ahead, and told the hotel only that morning to change the booking to a double room. He'd even postponed his trip to Nagpur to meet his parents, not wanting to miss out on time with Riya. Clearly, he'd been assuming more than he should have.

'You could go home, pick up some stuff and come back,' he suggested. 'The hotel's much closer to your office than your home is.'

Riya took a deep breath. 'I don't know, Dhruv,' she said honestly. 'I'm not comfortable moving in with you. I'm not even sure we should keep seeing each other.'

His brow furrowed. 'Is something wrong? Last night—' He broke off, not sure what he should say next. He'd consciously not brought up the argument they'd had in her flat, or the way she'd avoided him afterwards, not wanting to damage the newly forged connection between them. Probably he should have mentioned it—whatever had upset her then was clearly still on her mind.

Riya was pleating her napkin between her fingers and refusing to look up.

'I don't really know you that well any more, do I?' she blurted out. 'I don't know what movies you like, or what music you listen to or your favourite dessert—I don't even know what your favourite colour is!'

'If you stuck around long enough for us to talk, maybe you'd know,' Dhruv said drily. Seeing her flinch, he leaned forward, capturing one of her hands in his, and asked more gently, 'What's bothering you?'

'The last few days were wonderful,' she said unhappily. 'But this isn't practical. You live in Singapore, I don't plan to move out of India, and we don't even have much in common any more. We should probably end this before it gets any more serious.'

Before I get hurt again, she added silently to herself. *Before you tell me that, while the sex was great, you aren't in love with me. Before I agree to take this further and live the rest of my life in the hope that you'll start believing in love some day.*

Dhruv looked away from Riya for a few seconds. So far he hadn't really thought ahead—he enjoyed being with her, the sex was out of this world, and he'd assumed things would fall into place when they needed to. He hadn't even begun thinking about practicalities.

'Look, I'm not sure where you're going with this,' he said finally. 'We don't need to bring in a bunch of complications right now.' He gently ran a finger down her arm, not missing the little shiver of response that went through her. 'We're having a good time together— why cut it short? I'll be in Mumbai a lot now that we're setting up here. We can take our time getting to know each other better, and if things work out then we'll start worrying out about who stays where, hmm?'

Riya nodded. The restaurant was too public a place to argue in, and in any case he didn't look as if he'd get the point of what she was saying any time soon. She'd need to sort this out on her own, figure out how long she could bear being around him without permanent heart damage.

She stared down at her plate for a few seconds, and then said abruptly, 'I hate mushrooms,' pushing the few that were on her plate to the very edge.

Dhruv laughed. 'That's one step towards knowing you better, then,' he said. 'Any other foods that don't meet with your approval?'

'I hate yellow vegetables, too,' she said, frowning. She was being absurd, and a little childish, but she knew it was a side of her Dhruv was indulgent towards. Also, she didn't feel up to any more serious conversation. 'Pumpkins, especially. Actually, I hate all yellow things. Sunflowers. Canaries. Mustard. People with jaundice.'

'Least favourite colour—yellow. Noted,' Dhruv said mock-seriously. 'Favourite colour?'

'Red.'

'Ah, yes. Even your car's red, isn't it?'

'Yes, it was,' Riya said absently, and then, realising her lapse, 'I mean it *is*.'

Dhruv looked up quickly. 'What exactly has happened to your car?' he asked. 'You don't have it with you, and I heard you tell someone on the phone this morning that it's not at your apartment. Did you smash it up in an accident?'

Riya flushed angrily. 'No, I didn't! I sold it, OK? God, just because I drive a little fast...'

Dhruv ignored her indignation. 'Sold it—why? How do you plan to travel to work?'

'None of your business why I sold it,' Riya retorted. 'And I plan to take cabs to work—little black things with four wheels and yellow roofs? Heard of them?'

He frowned, saying, 'I thought you really loved that car, Riya?'

His voice was oddly gentle, and Riya felt close to tears. 'I needed the money,' she replied, in a voice so low that he could barely make out the words.

'I thought I'd offered to help you out,' he said slowly. 'This is about your parents, isn't it? And that old mausoleum of a house that's falling apart. Riya, there's no point pouring your money into that place. Better to pull it down and build something new, or sell the land and get a smaller place.'

Alongside the pure, elemental and completely physical lust that swamped Dhruv every time he looked at her, the sense that Riya needed to be taken care of was growing. She was an independent little spitfire, and she'd die before she asked for help, but there was too much on her plate. Her dad's health, the damage to her parents' house, her own flat unliveable in because of the floods, no car, a tyrannical boss—and he'd only scratched the surface. There were probably a million other things that she was trying to handle all on her own in her pig-headed, secretive and rather adorable way.

'It's not the house,' Riya said stonily, lying through her teeth. 'My sister's taking care of that. I've run up some debts, and the loan instalments on the car were getting difficult to keep up with.'

Dhruv frowned, but he didn't push the subject—to Riya's relief. The list of things she wanted to avoid discussing with him was growing very rapidly—soon the weather and the economic crisis would be the only safe topics of conversation.

They were mostly silent for the rest of the meal. Neither of them wanted dessert, so Dhruv asked for the bill. It had stopped raining, and the air outside smelt clean and earthy. There was a flower-seller on the pavement right outside the restaurant, and Riya stopped on impulse to buy a little garland of jasmine—the kind that older Maharashtrian women wore in their hair. The car pulled up just as she finished paying, and Dhruv held the door open for her.

'What are you going to do with that?' he asked, gesturing at the jasmine flowers she was still holding in her hands.

'I like the smell,' Riya said, lifting the garland to her nose and inhaling deeply. 'We had a jasmine shrub at home, and my mum used to use the flowers for *puja*.'

Dhruv didn't say anything, but his expression softened. In spite of her sophisticated exterior Riya was still very much a small-town girl. It was yet another of the things that drew him to her—the fact that she hadn't lost her connection with her roots.

In his own case, the bond with his parents had gone a long time ago—he still was a dutiful son, visiting them at least once a year, but he was always glad when the visits were over. The years of conflict between the two of them had left too deep a mark on him to want to rekindle the connection. Even when he was with Karan and Chutki the unpleasantness of shared memories made him want to limit his time with them. And they had moved so often because of his father's work that he didn't feel any kind of attachment to one place in particular. Or any person in particular, he thought with a jolt. Being with Riya was making him very conscious of how disconnected he'd become from the world.

A tall, grey-haired European man was stepping out of the hotel lift as Riya and Dhruv walked into the foyer. A smile of recognition crossed his face as he saw them. 'Riya!' he said, and then, looking at the keycard in her hand, 'I saw you here yesterday as well—have you moved in? I thought you lived somewhere in Parel?' He pronounced it Purr-rale.

'I'm here only for a few days, Pete,' Riya replied, cursing herself for having forgotten that her department head had rented an apartment in this same hotel for his one-year stint in India.

'With a friend, I see.' Pete Larsen smiled, holding his hand out to Dhruv. 'Malhotra, right? I haven't seen you in the gym since the first few days,' he said, and then, inclining his head in Riya's direction, 'Of course I'm sure you were otherwise occupied.'

Dhruv laughed and shook his hand, saying, 'I mean to be there tomorrow. I normally work out every day, but my schedule's gone for a toss ever since I met Riya.'

The two men started talking about the latest financial crisis while Riya writhed in an agony of embarrassment, almost shoving Dhruv into the lift when its doors opened the next time.

'Great—now my boss's boss knows that I sleep around,' she muttered as the lift doors closed. 'Won't that look good on my appraisal? I guess he'll put it under my "learning and growth" quadrant—an extra social skill I've acquired during the year.'

'Riya, he's Swedish,' Dhruv said patiently. 'I doubt he finds your sex-life particularly scandalous. Or un-usual.'

'Yes, but *I'm* Indian,' Riya said, her eyes flashing

up into his. '*I* find it scandalous and unusual. I'm not even planning to marry you—I don't know why I'm sleeping with you!'

'Don't you?' Dhruv asked, his voice dangerously quiet, and Riya looked into his golden eyes with misgiving.

He took her wrist as the lift stopped at their floor, almost pulling her to the door of their room. Once inside, he snapped on the light and turned on her, backing her up against the wall, his hands on either side of her.

'I'm tired of you treating me as some kind of guilty secret,' he said, his voice low but emphatic. 'I've been letting you be, thinking you were confused and needed some space, but this is the outside of enough.'

'If I treat you like a guilty secret, that's probably because you deserve to be treated like one,' Riya came back strongly. 'You're so out of touch with things in India you've no idea about what's acceptable and what's not. If you had any sense you wouldn't be expecting me to broadcast the fact that I'm sleeping with you.'

'And if you were the kind of Sati-Savitri you're making yourself out to be you wouldn't have been so willing to get into my bed in the first place,' Dhruv said, now seriously angry. 'Riya, we need to get some things straight. I'm not ashamed of what we have together, and if you are I suggest you think about it a little and figure out why. Whatever the reason is, it's got very little to do with me.' He took a deep breath, and pointed at her. '*You* have a set of ridiculous rules you live by—rules that are made by other people and that you don't believe in yourself. *You're* the one who is terrified of what other people will think. *You're* the one who wants every random person on the road to like you—so much so that you live to please them rather than yourself. You've changed, Riya, just as much as you say I have. And let me tell you most of the changes are for the worse.'

His anger seemed to be coming off him in waves, and Riya had to acknowledge the partial truth of what he said. It wasn't that she was afraid of gossip—she didn't really care all that much about what people thought of her. It was the thought of anyone else, even her family, knowing how much she cared for Dhruv that terrified her. Somehow it took the dream-like quality out of their relationship and made it very, very real.

Dhruv himself was completely oblivious to the fact that she was falling in love with him, but it would be evident even to a passing acquaintance. It would only compound the hurt when they actually did split up. Perhaps she was being stupidly optimistic, but if no one knew she still thought she might be able to deal with it.

She wasn't about to cede the argument to Dhruv though. 'Maybe you're right,' she acknowledged. 'I *do* bother about what other people think. I *do* want people to like me. And that's probably because I haven't grown into a swollen-headed, arrogant, prejudiced person like you.'

Dhruv's eyes narrowed. 'So now I'm swollen-headed?'

'And arrogant,' she added helpfully.

For the first time she had the feeling that she was really getting under Dhruv's skin—he was genuinely worked up, and the man-in-control mask was slipping fast. In spite of her own agitation, she found she was perversely enjoying baiting him—the old saw about women being more beautiful when they are angry applied to some men as well. Dhruv looked like a young Indra, his eyes flashing fire and his fair skin flushed.

His eyes narrowed even further. 'OK, arrogant, too. So I presume my being swollen-headed and arrogant is what *forces* you to keep the fact you're sleeping with me a closely guarded secret?'

Riya cocked her had to one side. 'No, I wouldn't say that,' she said. 'You'd already know this if you weren't so oblivious to the world around you. I don't want people to know because in India it's still considered shameful for unmarried people to be sleeping together. Even in Mumbai. I know you've been living overseas for a long while, but things here haven't changed all that much since we were teenagers.'

'Why sleep with me, then?' he asked, his eyes still dark with anger, but with a little tinge of vulnerability underneath.

'Because I couldn't help myself,' Riya said softly, leaning forward and kissing him gently on the lips.

His anger melted immediately, replaced by a surge of desire so strong that he almost flung her onto the bed, ripping off his own clothes and hers in a matter of seconds. Their lovemaking was fierce this time, with Riya raking her nails down his back, wilder and more passionate than she had ever been before, and Dhruv reining himself in just enough to avoid hurting her.

Both of them fell asleep almost immediately afterwards—too spent even to move an inch.

CHAPTER EIGHT

DHRUV woke up early, and looked at Riya sleeping quietly next to him. Her long lashes fluttered slightly, and she gave a little sigh and turned over in her sleep. She looked younger, and oddly defenceless, her long hair scattered around her, and her breathing so soft that her chest hardly moved.

In a fit of unusual tenderness, he gently moved a lock of hair off her face. In response she nestled closer, one small hand coming to rest on his thigh. Dhruv's body reacted immediately and he gave a small groan, pushing her hand off his leg and getting out of bed. Waking her up was a tempting idea, but he needed some time to himself to sort out his own thoughts.

He crossed the room, and stood at the window for a few minutes, looking out unseeingly at the lawns below. His behaviour the night before had been unforgivable—he had been so furious with Riya until she'd leaned forward and kissed him that he had been an inch away from physically grabbing her and shaking the living daylights out of her. More than anything else, what bothered him was the fact that she could make him lose control so easily—over his temper, his emotions, his life. For so many years he'd kept other people—especially women—at arm's length, but Riya had slipped under his defences effortlessly.

His lips curled in a mirthless smile. In spite of the sparks flying every time they met, he was very seriously considering marriage with her. Which probably made him all kinds of a fool. But the thought of an insipid arranged marriage now seemed almost unbearable.

Riya finally awoke at eight o'clock, sitting up and pushing her long hair back from her forehead. Dhruv was making coffee, and he turned around as he felt her gaze on his back.

'Sleep well?' he asked.

'Like a baby,' she said, smothering a yawn as she got out bed. She was wearing an old T-shirt of his, and her long legs were bare. Dhruv's eyes were automatically drawn towards them, and she blushed, pulling the hem down. 'I need to brush my teeth,' she muttered and, grabbing one of the sets of clothes she'd bought the day before, she made a dash for the bathroom.

Dhruv went back to making the coffee, a slight smile hovering on his lips. He found Riya's sudden bouts of shyness endearing. They were such a contrast with her eager, even demanding behaviour in bed.

She emerged from the bathroom ten minutes later and sat down at the table, pulling a mug of coffee towards her.

'Thank heavens today's Saturday,' she said. 'There's no way I could have hauled myself into work on time. I don't feel like moving.'

She peered into the coffee cup, inspecting the contents.

'Not strong enough,' she pronounced, and Dhruv reached back to get the tin of coffee. Taking it from him, she noticed a bite mark on his neck, and touched it apologetically. 'Sorry,' she said.

She looked so guilty that he laughed, pulling her to him and seating her on his lap. 'Don't be,' he said, nuzzling the nape of her neck. 'Last night was one of the best nights of my life.'

'Hmm,' Riya said, putting her coffee down on the table before she spilt it. 'Given what I've heard of your track record, I suppose I should feel honoured.'

'What would you know about my track record?' Dhruv asked, tugging at a lock of her hair.

Riya shrugged. 'Chutki said you've had dozens of girlfriends.'

'One day I'll strangle that little brat,' Dhruv said, only half joking. 'I've had exactly two girlfriends who've lasted more than six months, and it wasn't serious with either of them.'

Riya slid off his lap and picked up her coffee, to sip at it slowly. 'I've lasted almost a week,' she said lightly. 'Would that be a record?'

Dhruv looked up sharply. 'It's different with you, Riya. You know that,' he said.

'Do I?' Riya replied. 'Why? Because I'm Indian? Haven't you ever slept with an Indian girl before?' This time she was deliberately trying to goad him into losing his temper.

'It has absolutely nothing to do with your being Indian, and you know it!' Dhruv got up, running a hand through his hair in exasperation. 'You could be from Outer Mongolia for all I care. I've known you since you were seventeen, Riya. Do you think I'd get into a one-night stand with you?'

Riya looked up at him. 'I guess you wouldn't,' she

said. 'I'm sorry, Dhruv, it's just that I sometimes feel I don't know you at all. Everything's moved a bit too fast.'

The words echoed in Dhruv's brain for a while. He'd thought he was long beyond the stage where words could hurt him—surely his parents had cured him of that?—but after last night, if Riya could still say she didn't know him... His hands balled into fists by his sides, and he had to make a conscious effort to calm down.

'Let's take the time to get to know each other better, then,' he said carefully. 'I think I'll need to go to Nagpur for a few days next week, but when I'm back let's take things more slowly—try and understand each other a little better.'

'I'll be in Hong Kong next week,' Riya said.

'Work?' he asked. 'For how long?' He should have expected something like this, he thought bitterly. Riya was like quicksilver in his hands—just when he thought he had her figured out, she went off at a tangent.

'Three months at least—maybe longer.'

There was a pause while Dhruv digested this. He felt a little numb, though anger was beginning to stir. She must have known about the trip for a while, and she hadn't told him. If he hadn't forced his way back into her life she'd have left without a word to him. Part of him felt so betrayed, he wanted to kill her.

'Why didn't you mention this earlier?'

'It just came up a couple of days back,' she replied. 'And I wasn't even sure if we were going to continue seeing each other.'

'Let's assume that we were,' Dhruv said. 'I can't postpone my trip home any more, but we can probably meet in Hong Kong.'

Riya looked up at him in alarm. She'd thought long

and hard the night before, staring into the darkness for some hours after Dhruv had fallen asleep by her side, and the only conclusion she'd been able to come to had been that she needed to get away from Dhruv before he shattered her heart to smithereens. She'd finally accepted that she was in love with him—not *almost* in love, but stupidly, thoroughly and irredeemably in love. She wasn't sure what had tipped the balance, but it was done now. No going back. Getting out with her heart intact was no longer an option, but she could try and limit the damage.

Some of her alarm must have shown in her face, because Dhruv raised his eyebrows. 'From your expression I gather you're not thrilled by the thought,' he said. 'But think about it. If you really believe that we need to spend more time together to figure out things between us, this is the ideal opportunity. No one knows you in Hong Kong, so you won't need to bother about your "reputation…"'

Riya flushed angrily at the almost visible quotation marks around the word.

He continued ruthlessly. 'And it's easy for me to work from there for a while—my moving to Mumbai can always be postponed. The only thing against it is that you're scared.'

'I'm not scared!' Riya retorted.

'Right.'

'I'm *not*!' she said. But she was. Not scared for the reasons that he meant, but scared that she was getting into this too deep—scared that she wouldn't be able to get out without getting hurt. And most of all scared because even though she'd given him her heart she couldn't trust him—not after the way he'd treated her so many years ago.

'You leave for Hong Kong next week, right?' Dhruv asked, his gaze challenging. 'I have a project running there that's due for a review—I could come over after a couple of weeks.'

Riya took a deep breath. 'But what would be the point, Dhruv?' she asked. 'I don't really see a future for us together—and we're arguing more and more... Why don't we just call it quits and move on? You're looking to get married—the longer we stay together, the more your settling down gets postponed.'

Dhruv looked stunned. 'Do you actually think I'd go through with an arranged marriage after *this,* Riya?' he asked. 'My God, if that's the kind of person you think I am, I'm not surprised you want to get away from me as quickly as you can.'

Riya looked away, not wanting to answer.

Dhruv paced the room, his frustration building as the silence stretched on. He wanted Riya so badly he could hardly think straight, and her resistance was driving him up the wall. He wasn't sure what she wanted—commitment, promises, marriage? Whatever it was, it was incomprehensible to him. All he knew was that he'd lose her if he didn't do something, and the thought shook him up more than he could have imagined.

He stopped by Riya's side, his mind suddenly made up. If commitment was what she was looking for, that at least was something he was ready to offer.

'Would knowing that I want to marry you change anything?' he asked, his voice completely flat as he tried to keep it devoid of emotion.

Riya felt her heart give a loud, uneven thump.

'Why?' she asked. 'Why do you want to marry me?'

'We get on well together. I have a lot of respect for

you. The sex is amazing. What more could I want from someone I marry?'

'But you're not in love with me, are you?' she asked, her eyes challenging as she held his gaze. It was so tempting to agree, to let those steady golden eyes beguile her into saying yes. Only a very strong effort of will made her keep questioning his motives.

Dhruv shook his head slowly. 'I don't think I'm the kind of person who falls in love, Riya,' he said. 'I don't believe in it. I never have.'

His expression showed that he meant every word of what he said, and Riya felt her heart break a little as she made up her mind.

'Marriage doesn't work for me, then,' she said.

Dhruv raised his eyebrows. 'Why is that?' he asked, not fully believing what he was hearing. He wasn't the kind of man who took pride in his conquests, but he had been with enough women to realise that marriage to him was a fairly attractive proposition. And Riya was definitely not indifferent to him—he'd have expected her to at least consider the offer, not reject it out of hand.

'We want very different things from marriage, Dhruv,' she said. 'You're looking for something like a business arrangement, and that's not what I want. Look at the way you proposed—if you call that a proposal. It sounded more like you were hiring me to work for you, putting me on probation till you made the offer permanent.' She wrinkled her nose. 'And it wasn't even a very appealing offer—what exactly *are* you offering, other than good sex?'

'What is it that you want?'

'Much, much more,' she said firmly. 'I agree that I'm crazily attracted to you, but...' *deep breath* '...that's not enough. When I get married I want the man I marry to be in love with me. I want to be the centre of his world, someone he can't live without.'

His face had that familiar shuttered expression, but he was seething inside. Being told he wasn't good enough for marriage was a new experience, and it wasn't one he was particularly relishing. It wasn't just his vanity that had taken a beating—he did genuinely care for Riya more than he had cared for any woman before, and her offhand dismissal had hit deep. Only his clenched fists showed how close to losing his temper he was.

'So, unless I lie to you and tell you that I'm in love with you, you won't consider marriage—is that it?' he asked.

'Unless you are *really* in love with me,' Riya countered. 'I don't want you lying to me.'

'Oh, I'm a very good liar,' he drawled carefully. 'I doubt you'd be able to tell the difference. But I find that I don't feel like making the effort.'

Riya winced. She was very conscious of the fact that Dhruv's feelings for her were not as deep as hers, but having it spelt out so plainly still hurt.

Dhruv's anger dissolved when he saw her expression. Evidently his instinct was right, and she was nowhere as indifferent as she was pretending to be.

'I'd say you should think it out before you refuse definitely, Riya,' he said slowly. 'You're not seventeen any more, and it's time you outgrew childish notions of love and marriage. We're good in bed together and I like you—I assume you like me as well. You'd have a comfortable life with me—especially if you have money problems—you won't even need to work any more if you don't want to.'

Riya turned on him, her eyes blazing. 'Are you suggesting I'd marry you for *money*?' she demanded. 'How arrogant can you get, Dhruv? That's probably the most insulting thing anyone has ever said to me in my life.'

'Money is a factor for most women when they're choosing a husband,' Dhruv replied, the indifferent tone in which he spoke further fuelling her anger. 'You can choose to take it as an insult to womankind, but it's the truth.'

'Not for me.' Riya was so angry now she was almost in tears. 'I have to give it to you, Dhruv. Just when I think we've got to a stage where we can at least have a semi-civilised conversation you manage to do something to make me hate you again. What makes you think you can buy me like that?'

Dhruv's voice was chilly as he replied, 'I was making a very practical suggestion, Riya. Buying and selling doesn't come into it. You told me yourself that you've had to sell your car because you needed the money. Your parents aren't doing well financially, either. You work hard, but you don't have much to show for it. All I'm pointing out to you is that life would be simpler if you were married to me.'

Riya was shaking her head vigorously as he spoke. 'You don't know the first thing about me, Dhruv,' she said. 'I'd…I'd prefer cleaning rubbish dumps for a living to marrying someone who doesn't care about me. Even if I loved you, I wouldn't take a *paisa* from you.' Tears finally welled into her eyes, and she turned away with a loud sniff.

Finally realising how deeply he'd hurt her, Dhruv put his hands on her shoulders. 'Riya, you're misinterpreting everything I'm saying. I *do* care about you—or at least I care as much as I am able to care about anyone. I respect you, and…' He smiled a little, though the smile didn't reach his eyes fully. 'And I guess I don't need to tell you that I'm very strongly attracted to you.'

Riya took his hands off her shoulders and moved away, scrubbing at the tear marks on her face. His reference to caring about her to the extent that he could care about anyone had touched her deeply. If he hadn't talked about money earlier she'd have been tempted to agree to marriage just in the hope that he'd come to love her in time.

'It's not enough, Dhruv,' she said in a low voice.

'*What* isn't enough, goddamn it?' Dhruv asked, beginning to lose his temper again.

The conversation was taking on a nightmarish quality, and he had the sensation that he was banging his head against a velvet-cloaked concrete wall, knowing there was a door nearby but not being able to locate it. He'd never wanted a woman as much as he wanted Riya, and he knew she wanted him, too, but he just wasn't able to get through to her.

'The kind of marriage you're talking about.'

Dhruv stood up, putting his hands firmly on the table. 'If that's the way you feel, I guess there's nothing further we need to discuss,' he said.

He tried to tell himself that that this was some hard-to-get ploy, and if he called her bluff she'd come running back to him, but at heart he knew that wasn't the case. Riya looked genuinely distressed, and her next words proved that the thought of playing games with him hadn't even crossed her mind.

'I guess not,' she said. 'This is it, then.'

Her words were soft, though she felt as if she was coming apart. However much she loved Dhruv, there was no chance in hell he'd ever love her back. Willing herself not to burst into tears before she left the room, she walked across to the cupboard where her clothes were and started piling them together.

Dhruv came up behind her. 'If your flat doesn't have power yet you can stay on here,' he said, the words coming out sounding stilted.

Riya shook her head. 'I'll move into a friend's place if I have to,' she said.

She didn't have a bag. Dhruv silently handed her a rucksack, and she shoved her clothes into it all higgledy-piggledy. The watch he'd given her was lying on a shelf and she picked it up, wanting to return it to him. She turned around with it in her hand, but he closed her fingers around it without a word. Something in his expression told her not to give the watch back to him, and she slipped it into the bag along with her clothes.

'We could still be friends,' she suggested as she walked to the door. She regretted the words as soon as they were out of her mouth. It was an admission of weakness, telling Dhruv that she still wanted to be in touch with him.

Dhruv shook his head. 'I don't think so,' he said. 'If we're saying goodbye, this time it should be for good.'

Riya nodded mutely. This time her heart very definitely seemed to be breaking, and the detachment she'd tried to maintain over the last few days was deserting her very quickly. Her hand was on the doorknob, but she turned quickly and put her free arm around his neck to drag his lips down to hers. His hands came up to span her waist, but with a little sob she broke away from him and opened the door, almost running out in her hurry to get away.

CHAPTER NINE

DHRUV watched the door shut behind Riya, feeling emptier than he had ever before felt in his life. It would have been so easy to make her stay. Just a small lie. He'd lied many times before in his life—to his parents, to people he worked with, even to his sister. Usually to get something done. Sometimes to prevent someone from getting hurt. He hadn't been able to bring himself to lie to Riya, though—it would have seemed like a desecration, a betrayal of all they had between them.

He had always been very sure that he wasn't capable of love. Even his feelings for his family were ambivalent—he was fond of Chutki, and felt responsible for her, but Karan was more of a friend than a brother. He was almost completely indifferent to his parents. He felt all knotted up when he thought of Riya, though. He wanted to help her. She'd refused to confide in him, but he knew that her financial troubles weren't as simple as she made them out to be. He wanted to have her back in his bed. And he wanted to be with her for the rest of his life—laughing with her, having children with her, growing old with her. But that was possible only if he said he loved her, and he couldn't bring himself to utter that lie.

* * *

In Nagpur two days later he watched impassively as his parents got into yet another row. Chutki was sitting in her room, pretending to study, but he knew she was listening to every word. Karan had flown out again—he was needed back on his Kenyan project, and hadn't wanted to spend more time at home than strictly necessary. When the quarrel grew beyond a certain point Dhruv got to his feet, and strolled into another room.

He knew he could stop it whenever he wanted. He had always been his mother's favourite, and even his father had begun according him a grudging sort of respect ever since he had become a successful man in his own right. One word from him would force them into an uneasy truce, one that would last till exactly the minute he stepped out of the house and caught his flight back to Mumbai. But he found he couldn't be bothered.

Passing Chutki's room, he saw the girl staring into space, tightly clutching the textbook on her lap but not reading it. Concerned, he stepped into the room, and saw that large tears were rolling down her face.

'What's the matter?' he asked, putting a hand on her shoulder.

'I hate it,' she whispered. 'I hate it when they fight. It makes me sick.' And she did look ill—physically ill—a far cry from the bubbly, confident girl he'd always known.

Not normally very demonstrative with his siblings, he put an awkward arm around her shoulders.

She shrugged it off. '*You* don't care,' she said, turning away from him. 'You don't care and Karan doesn't care.'

'I care about you, *chhoti*,' he said gently, but she shook her head vigorously, scrubbing at her cheeks.

'No, you don't. You throw expensive gifts at me, but if I want to tell you about something that's bothering me you don't stop to listen. You're like that with everyone. Just like Papa. If you ever get married you'll treat your wife like she's some kind of showpiece—not a living, breathing person. I pity the girl, whoever she is.'

She gave a loud sniff and turned to her book, but Dhruv stared at her, transfixed. If that was what his own sister thought of him, no wonder he hadn't been able to convince Riya to marry him. Now that he thought back, he hadn't really tried convincing her. He'd just expected her to fall into his arms as soon as he said the word. And when she hadn't he'd tried bribing her—ugly as it sounded, that was exactly what he'd done. He'd not tried to find out *why* she was short of money, or if she was in any kind of trouble. He'd thrown money at the problem and been angry when she'd thrown it back in his face.

A second sniff from Chutki drew him back to the immediate issue at hand, and he went swiftly back to the living room, where his mother was now watching TV silently and his father had hidden himself behind a newspaper. He took the remote from his mother's un-resisting hands, clicked it off and began to talk.

It hadn't been easy, he mused two days later, during his flight back to Mumbai, but he was glad he'd taken a stance rather than being an indifferent bystander while his parents tore his sister apart with their ceaseless quarrels. He'd not tried to reason with his parents. He'd just told them quietly that Chutki was finding it difficult to deal with their constant bickering, and he'd be taking her to Mumbai with him for the next academic session. It was unlikely that either of them would be back to visit once they'd left.

That had been enough to get them to stop and take a long, hard look at their lives and their marriage—now they were going off on a holiday to Europe together to try and sort out their problems. He was under no illusions that they'd improve, but he'd redeemed himself at least partially in Chutki's eyes. She'd agreed to stay back with their parents when her mother had begged her to, but she'd been ecstatic at Dhruv's offering to take her with him to Mumbai. Her *bhaiya* was again her hero, the way he had been when she was eight years old.

He smiled as he thought of his sister. It would have turned his life upside down if she had decided to come and stay with him, but he found that he was prepared to handle the turmoil as long as she was happy. He hadn't realised how much his sister meant to him—and how important her opinion of him was. She'd opened up a lot more with him and, while he'd not been able to bring himself to discuss Riya with her, had sensed that something was troubling him. She had been sweetly sympathetic without being nosy. A lot like the way she'd been as a child, he thought, remembering the way she'd clambered onto his lap and hugged him when he'd come back home after graduation. His parents still hadn't been speaking to each other then, and he'd just broken up with Riya. Life had seemed very bleak.

Life still seemed very bleak without Riya. He had been unable to put her out of his head—if anything, she filled his thoughts more with each passing day. He had played their last conversation over and over again in his mind, and in hindsight realised that things had spun out of control the second he'd said he wasn't in love with her. And then he'd compounded it by talking about money, which seemed to be very sore point with Riya.

He frowned, trying to remember if she'd been like that in college. No, she hadn't, he decided finally, but in college both of them had been students, living on shoestring allowances. Even then his parents had probably been a lot better off than hers, but it would have been less apparent given that they'd stayed in a different city.

He rubbed his forehead. None of this was helping. The basic fact remained that Riya didn't want a man who didn't love her. She'd have probably let him down a little more gently if he hadn't tried 'buying' her into marriage, but she wouldn't have married him all the same. He was unsure now about his own feelings, unable to label and compartmentalise them the way he had earlier. What he felt for Riya was too strong to go under a standard label like lust, or affection or infatuation. If anything, being in love described his current condition the best.

The more he thought about it, the more he thought he'd been at fault. He'd been arrogant, assuming she'd fall into his arms if he crooked his little finger. It had felt so right being with her that he'd dismissed all her misgivings without a thought, barrelling into her life and into her bed without giving her space to think. And now that she was gone he was beginning to realise that he couldn't do without her.

Half a continent away, after finally dragging the last of her bags off the conveyor belt, Riya wheeled her trolley to a corner of the busy airport and dug out her phone to call Melissa. The past few days in the office had been crazy. She'd only just about managed to catch her flight to Hong Kong, and now she'd realised that the printout with her hotel details had got left behind on the flight. The miserable state of mind she'd been in ever since she'd walked out of Dhruv's door still persisted, and she wished she could just catch a flight back to India and go home to her parents.

'Do I need to take the Airport Express, or is there a car waiting for me?' she asked, once Melissa had dictated the address of the hotel.

'There should be a car,' Melissa replied.

It took her some time to find it—it was booked under the company's name, and the car rental company spent ages finding the records and locating her driver. Finally, a cheerful-looking Chinese man hurried into the terminal, carrying a placard with her name on it—he'd also been given incorrect instructions, and had been waiting in the wrong part of the airport.

The drive from the airport to Hong Kong Island was a long one. Riya gazed out of the window all the way, entranced by the sights outside, but at the same time missing Dhruv acutely. The skyline was amazing, with the Bank of China building dwarfing the others around it, and Riya felt a pang as she remembered Dhruv telling her about one of the buildings he was working on in Singapore. Maybe it would be as imposing as this one, she thought.

She'd done a Google search on his business partner Krish's work, and it was impressive—buildings stark and modern in design, but with the kind of beauty that would endure. She'd checked out some of Dhruv's work, too, though she'd felt a little guilty doing so, as if she was snooping on him. His forte was designing simple structures that were beautiful, but worked, and made the best use of the materials at hand—a style of architecture that was far more suited to a country like India than Krish's more flamboyant designs. In some ways she found she preferred his work to Krish's. It was so much more grounded and real.

She wished she'd got a chance to tell him so before they'd parted. One of the things that had bothered her was that he was now totally focused on the business side of his work and had given up doing any designing. Not that he'd have paid any attention even if she *had* told him, she thought with a sigh as the car pulled up in front of her hotel—nothing he'd said to her led her to believe he valued her opinion in any way.

Her room was tiny, even by Mumbai standards, with barely enough space for a bed and a TV with a couch in front. Riya went to the large windows and pulled back the curtains to look out. The hotel was quite high up on the hill, and she could see the city spread out in front of her. She didn't need to go to work till the next day and, while she was tired, she felt too strung out to go to sleep. There was a limit to the amount of time she could spend obsessing about Dhruv. A nice brisk walk seemed the answer, and she slipped on her shoes and let herself out.

It was still warm, and the sky was clear, though the weather updates she'd read before leaving India had said that this was typhoon season in Hong Kong. The hotel she was staying in was in the Mid-Levels, halfway up the slopes of the island. Riya wasn't sure if she'd be able to find her way back—all the blocks looked similar—so she walked to a park from which she could see the apartments. Everything was very clean, but somehow aseptic—without character. She'd already started missing Mumbai, with all its dirt and clutter.

Leaning back on a park bench, Riya looked up at the cloudless sky. She was in a strange mood—life seemed to be in limbo. Away from India and the confined circle of her life there she felt free. Of course there was the office to go to, and the work here was not likely to be very different or very much more exciting than it was in India.

Once again she felt a pang at not being with Dhruv. This would have been her chance to spend unfettered time with him. She wouldn't have had to bother about her parents finding out or her colleagues passing remarks behind her back. She could have enjoyed three months with him, and when the time had come to go back she'd have been able to move on—hopefully with not too many regrets. They might even have reached some kind of middle ground and decided to get married.

Her heart stuttered a little at the thought. If only he hadn't brought money up, she thought, brushing angry tears away from her eyes. It had cheapened the whole thing, made her feel as if he thought of her as someone who could be bought.

The sun was setting and it was getting slightly chilly when Riya finally got up to retrace her path back to the hotel. She felt more peaceful, having thought long and hard about Dhruv. She'd finally come to terms with the fact that while she was in love with him, her love would never be returned. The thought hurt, but in the larger scheme of things it wasn't a tragedy. Marrying him when he didn't love her would have been—she'd have spent the rest of her life expecting something out of him that he wasn't able to give, and it would have destroyed her. As things were… Maybe she wasn't perfectly happy, but in the last few hours she'd passed the self-pity stage and was ready to get on with life. She was also trying to be mature about her time with him, sifting through her memories to choose the best ones to hold on to and discard the rest. The memory of him offering her money was the one that rankled the most, try as she might to tell herself that he looked at things differently, so she decided to shove that to the back of her head and not think about it.

It wasn't as simple as it sounded, of course, and she still went through several bouts of utter misery over the next few weeks—especially when she came back from a hard day's work to the empty, cramped hotel room, and would have given anything to have Dhruv by her side, if only for a few minutes. However, she managed to restrain herself from calling him up—that chapter of her life was definitely closed now.

The only weakness she allowed herself was wearing the watch he'd given her night and day, taking it off only when she went for a bath. It was the only thing he had ever given her—she didn't even have a proper photograph of him, only the few group photographs that had been taken at Gaurav's wedding. The expression in his eyes when she had made a move to give it back to him had made her think for a moment that in spite of his saying that he didn't 'do' love at some level he genuinely cared for her. It would be a dangerous thought, if allowed to flower, but she was careful not to build on it too much.

CHAPTER TEN

RIYA'S first month in Hong Kong passed quickly, the heavy workload keeping her mind off her troubles. On weekends she went on long cycling and trekking trips in the surrounding islands—sometimes with friends she'd made in the client's office, but mostly alone. For the first time in her life solitude didn't bother her.

She'd been in regular touch with her parents, and e-mailing her sister on and off to get news. Her parents were still staying with Shreya, and Riya called them once a week. She'd restricted the frequency because her parents were of the generation that thought international calls should be made only when there was death or serious illness. They were clearly so uncomfortable at the thought of the bill she was running up that in the end she had told them that her company reimbursed one call a week—a lie similar to the one she'd told them about her insurance covering her father's medical expenses, when actually she'd paid them out of her own pocket.

Looking through her bank statements on the internet a few days into October, Riya realised that the cheque she'd given her mother still hadn't been cleared. She frowned as she tried to puzzle things out. There were enough funds in her account, so the cheque couldn't have bounced.

She finally called, telling Shreya as soon as she picked up the phone, 'Tell Mum that I'm adjusting this call against next week's. I don't want her getting all worked up about how much it's costing me.'

Shreya laughed, and handed their mother the phone.

'Dhruv did *what*?' Riya asked five minutes later, not sure if she'd heard her mother right.

Her mother sounded a little bewildered at the sharpness of Riya's tone. 'But, *beta,* didn't he tell you?' she asked. 'He sent this nice boy across—he's a contractor, I think, or maybe an architect—they used to study together. Anyway, he took a look at the house and he said he'll be able to fix it. It'll be much cheaper than what the man your father spoke to said. And he was saying that if we want he can buy the property from us and give us a flat in this new complex he's developed.'

'Dad wouldn't agree to that, would he?' Riya asked.

Her mother sniffed. 'He wouldn't have if someone had suggested it years ago, but now he has. He finds the stairs difficult to manage, and a ground-floor flat would be much more convenient. And it's not like you or Shreya will ever come and live here—you'll probably settle down in Mumbai anyway. There's no point in hanging on to the house for sentimental reasons. Better that we sell the place and be less of a burden on you financially.'

Riya flared up. 'You're not a burden! Did this "nice" boy put this rubbish into your head?'

'No, he didn't,' her mother said tartly. 'If you really want to know, I'm sick of living in this house, wondering when it'll collapse around my ears. We needed the space when you and Shreya were little, but your dad and I can manage perfectly well in a two-bedroom flat—and I won't have to spend half the day dusting and cleaning. The new complex is nice—it has a senior citizens' club, and it's very near Shreya's clinic. She can drop Aryan off with me when she's at work.'

Riya had never heard her mother sound quite so emphatic in a while. She felt a little guilty about not having figured out in so many years that her mother wasn't happy with the house. Her mum could have told her, of course, she thought defensively, but then, when had her mother ever complained about anything?

'So, this Dhruv boy,' her mother began, taking up a new tack.

'He's not a boy, exactly, Mum. He's three years older than me.'

'Which means he's a boy as far as I'm concerned,' her mother said firmly. 'Don't try to change the topic, Riya. Is he the same one you used to spend so much time with when you were at college?'

'Yes, Mum.' There was no point trying to hide anything from her mother. She was a human ferret when it came to digging out secrets that concerned her family.

'So, do you like him?' her mother persisted. 'Shreya thought there might be something happening.'

Thinking to herself that she'd like to throttle her sister the next time she met her, Riya replied, 'No, Mum, it's not like that.'

'But you used to really like him,' her mother said. 'You were so upset when he left. We were really worried about you.'

'You knew?' Riya asked, not even surprised any longer. Her mother probably knew how many times she had kissed Dhruv, and where, and the exact circumstances under which he had dumped her.

'Of course we did, *beta*. You used to sit and write "Riya Malhotra" on the last pages of all your notebooks, and then tear them out and shred them. And the whole college was talking about the two of you—even the principal's wife mentioned it to me.'

'I'm so glad I don't live at home any more,' Riya muttered.

'Actually, so am I,' her mother said briskly. 'Small-town life didn't suit you. You're better off in Mumbai. Not like Shreya. She loves it here. But you need to get married and settle down. There are some girls who're happy on their own, but you're not one of them. If it's not working with Dhruv, find someone else you like.'

A sudden thought struck Riya. 'Mum, have you met Dhruv?' she asked. 'Recently I mean?'

Her mother hesitated and then said, 'Yes—that's when he put this architect in touch with us. He'd come down to speak to the principal of your old college about some project they're doing. Something about housing for villagers. Suitable housing or susceptible housing—something like that.'

'Sustainable housing,' Riya said impatiently. Dhruv had mentioned the project briefly. 'What else did he say, Mum?'

'Something about a green architecture course that they're introducing in the college—he's going to send some material across to the professors. And, of course, he's setting up an office in India. Oh—and you didn't tell me he was Gaurav's cousin? They look nothing like each other—Gaurav's such a nice boy, but he isn't anywhere as good-looking as Dhruv. They're both tall, of course...'

Some of Riya's tenseness must have communicated itself to her mother, because she relented and said in gentler tones, 'We didn't talk about you, *beta*. He said he'd met you in Mumbai, but that's all.'

Thank heavens for that. Not that she'd expected Dhruv to discuss her, but her mother could draw information out of a clam. And Dhruv had always liked her mum, even though he'd met her only a few times while they were in college.

Wanting to know more, but not wanting to tip her mother off, she hesitated a little before she asked the next question. But her mother got in first.

'Gaurav told us that you sold your car,' she said reprovingly. 'Why didn't you tell us, Riya?'

Riya mumbled something, wishing she could get her hands on Gaurav.

Her mum, with her uncanny ability to read her children's thoughts, said immediately, 'Now, don't you say anything to him. I'm glad he told us. I've asked him to go and speak to that Rishabh boy and get it back immediately. I never liked Rishabh anyway.'

'But, Mum!' Riya said in horror. 'Who's going to pay for it?'

'I am,' her mother said firmly. 'We've got the first instalment for the house already, and I've transferred it to Gaurav. Did it online, too,' she added proudly.

'You've sold the house already?' Riya asked, her voice shaking a little. She'd grown up in that house, and she realised suddenly that, more than her dad, *she* was the one who'd wanted to cling on to it no matter what.

'They won't start working on it till you come back, Riya,' her mother said gently. 'And we can change our mind and give the money back any time before December. If that's what you want. But look at it practically, *beta*. We can't depend on you for ever—you know how your father is. Once you get married, he won't take a rupee from you. Shreya's been offering to help out for so long, but he refuses to listen to her.'

'You never told me you hated the house,' Riya said childishly.

'I used to have to scrub it from top to bottom twice a day when your grandmother was still alive,' her mum said. 'She didn't believe in hiring maids when there was a daughter-in-law around to do the work.'

Riya frowned. She was learning a lot about her mother today. She vaguely remembered her grand-mother, a benevolent white-haired lady who'd patted her on the head and fed her *jalebis* and cream, and she'd always thought that she and her mum got along really well.

'Didn't you like Daadiji, then?' she asked tentatively.

'Of course I did,' her mother said briskly. 'She was a pain sometimes, but she was a good person at heart. *Chalo,* you put the phone down now. Your company won't pay for an hour-long call.'

Riya said goodbye and rang off, chewing her lip thoughtfully. She was surprised that Dhruv had made the effort to seek out her parents. He'd come home a couple of times when they were in college, and had got along reasonably well with her parents, but she hadn't expected him to go and meet them—especially after what had happened in Mumbai. He'd fixed her money problems, though, more effectively and permanently than she would have been able to. And he'd done it without offering her or her parents money, she realised, the small tinge of annoyance at his interference going away. So maybe some of what she'd said had actually hit home.

A small frisson of hope ran through her, but she suppressed it firmly.

* * *

The rest of the week was uneventful, and Riya woke up on Saturday feeling oddly restless. She didn't have anything planned for the day—she'd originally intended to laze around and relax, perhaps go for a swim, but the feeling of wanting to go out and 'do' something was too strong to resist. Not normally a 'touristy' person, she had left all her souvenir shopping for last, and it seemed a good idea to get it done with. She made a little face and pulled out her trusty *Lonely Planet* book. Stanley Market seemed to be the best option, so she slipped into a pair of shorts and comfortable shoes and trudged off to Exchange Square to catch a bus.

The market was enchanting, though very touristy, and Riya wandered around for hours, picking up gifts for her parents, sister and nephew, and a lot of small trinkets for people in the office. For herself she picked up a silk *cheong-sam* in midnight-blue, with a traditional plum flower and bamboo motif. It reached to mid-calf and was slit high. She wasn't sure when she'd ever wear it, but she bought it all the same.

Around one o'clock, loaded with bags, she wandered into one of the restaurants in Murray House and sat down to order a meal. It was when she opened her bag to pay the bill that she realised that there were three missed calls on her phone. All of them were from Dhruv.

For a few seconds she kept staring at the display, wondering if she was reading it right. A waiter came up to the table and she absently handed him her credit card, completely lost in thought. The call register showed that Dhruv had called once in the morning, around the time when she'd got onto the bus, and twice more in quick succession during the time she'd been winding up in the market. She wouldn't have heard it ring—partly because the market was noisy, and partly because she'd not used the phone much since she came to Hong Kong. It was too expensive to make calls from an India number, and it was only likely that her family would call her in an emergency.

Getting into the bus with her various parcels and packages, she frowned at the phone again. Why would he be calling? He'd said quite clearly when she'd left his apartment that it was best if they didn't stay in touch.

There was only one way to find out, Riya thought grimly as she tapped the touchscreen of her phone to call him back. He picked up on the second ring.

'Riya,' he said, and the sound of her name in those caressing tones sent little shivers of pleasure up her spine.

She shook herself.

'You called,' she said guardedly. There was no point letting him know how thrilled she was to hear his voice again. For all she knew he was calling to let her know that he'd decided to enter into holy matrimony with one of the Priyas, Preetis or Premas that his Seema Chachi had picked out for him. She'd look a right idiot if she gushed all over him.

'You aren't at your hotel, are you?' Dhruv asked. 'I tried calling there a couple of times before I tried your cell phone.'

'Went shopping,' Riya replied, not trusting herself to speak in full sentences, but wanting to know how he'd got her hotel number. Her parents, most likely, she realised, or Gaurav. Even if they had just told him the name of the hotel it would have been easy enough to find the number.

'Tsim Tsa Tsui?' he asked, mentioning the crowded area in Kowloon that lay just across the bay from Hong Kong Island.

'Stanley Market,' Riya replied, sticking doggedly to her two-word rule.

'Hmm—nice place,' Dhruv said, leading Riya to wonder hysterically if he would ever get to the point. She didn't answer, and he continued. 'I know you're wondering why I called. I'll come to the point quickly. I want you to give us another chance.' He went on before she could do more than make an inarticulate noise. 'I know I handled things badly, but I'll try and make it up to you if you're willing to forgive me.'

'No,' she said baldly—and so loudly that several people in the bus turned around to look at her.

'Why, Riya?'

'Because I deserve more,' Riya said hurriedly, very conscious of all the listening ears around her.

'I can't hear you clearly,' he said, the frustration in his voice mounting. 'You're mumbling, and there's a lot of background noise. Are you in a cab?'

'Bus,' she said. 'Wait a minute.'

The bus had stopped at Repulse Bay, and she got off, walking a little way onto the beach.

'I'm off the bus,' she said. 'Can you hear me clearly now?'

'Did you just get off in the middle of nowhere?' Dhruv asked, that disapproving tone she hated strong in his voice.

'I got off at a very nice beach, thank you very much,' she snapped. 'I'll catch the next bus back.'

'I didn't hear what you said earlier.'

'I said I deserve more,' Riya snapped out. 'I was in love with you when I was seventeen.' She cut him off ruthlessly when he started to say something. 'You listen to me this time, Dhruv. There's a lot I want to tell you, and it's easier to say on the phone. So I'm going to say it, and then I'm never going to speak to you again.'

Courage firmly in both hands, she plonked herself down on a bench with her purchases scattered around her.

'So, as I was saying, I was in love with you when I was seventeen—and don't you dare it say it was just a crush.'

'I wasn't going to say anything,' Dhruv said, very meekly by his standards.

'Stop interrupting,' Riya said fretfully. 'It's tough enough to say all this without you chiming in every minute like a cuckoo in a clock. What was I telling you?'

'That you loved me when you were seventeen.'

'I was. And it took me years to get over you. Even then I used to unconsciously compare every man I met with you. Then I met you again, and, like a mutt, I fell for you all over again.' She paused for a second, but he was silent. 'In the beginning I thought it was just infatuation, but I was wrong. I've been falling in love with you since the day I met you again. I'm not sure why. I don't trust you. I don't even like you always. In fact, I'm quite sure I hate you at times. But I know that I've never felt like this about anyone before, and I probably never will.'

She sniffed and rubbed at her eyes.

'One of the things I do like about you is that you're honest. You never pretended you were in love with me, and at first I thought it was OK—we'd have a short fling and I'd put it down to experience and carry on. But it wasn't that easy. I still think about you every day, and it still hurts, however hard I pretend to myself that it doesn't. And that's why I don't want to give it another chance. I'd take one look at you and forget all that I'm saying and fall into your arms. I've missed you so much I'd probably agree to whatever cold-blooded scheme you're suggesting this time—marriage or an affair— and either way you'd end up breaking my heart. Into tiny little pieces.'

He stayed silent.

Riya said gruffly, 'So that's it. I told you before. I think I deserve far more than a husband who's just marrying me to settle down and start a dynasty or whatever. I deserve a man who'll love me more than anything else, who'll be with me at all times, and who will respect me and not offer me money whenever I don't agree with him.' She knew the last dig was grossly unfair, but she continued anyway. 'And I want to marry him, and have three fat little babies. And I want to live a simple, normal life and be happy.'

Dhruv still didn't say anything.

'Does that explain how I feel?' she asked.

'It does,' he said slowly, and his voice didn't sound angry the way she'd expected it to, but resigned, and a little wistful. 'You're right. You do deserve a lot more than what I was offering you. I hope you find the man of your dreams, Riya, and I hope he's someone you can love as much as he loves you.'

And then he put the phone down.

Riya stared at the phone. 'So that's that,' she said, and got up from the bench to walk towards the beach, pretending that the reason her eyes were watering was that the breeze was really strong.

'Missee, your bags,' a little boy called out behind her, and she went back to pick up the assorted packages she'd picked up at the market.

She sat on the beach for a long while, watching the

tide come in. Dhruv had hit the weak spot in her plan when he'd said she hoped she'd love her mythical husband as much as he loved her. Because that was the problem, wasn't it? There had been men in her life who fitted the description she'd given Dhruv—uncomplicated, decent chaps who'd loved her. Vinay, her ex-fiancé, had been one, and there had been a colleague in CYB who had proposed marriage more than once. Even now Sudeep, one of the men she was working with in Hong Kong, had made it clear that he liked her. She could have married any one of them and they'd have given her the life she'd described to Dhruv. It was her own heart that balked at the thought of marrying any man other than Dhruv.

Maybe she was a one-man woman, she thought wryly. Like the birds who mated for life and pined away if their mate died. Or a masochist who liked the thought of being in love with a man who periodically stomped over her heart in thick boots. She could always stay single, of course. Move to a country where old maids were more common than they were in India, and where people didn't seem to think it was the bounden duty of every single person to get married and contribute to the population explosion.

The beach was relatively deserted, and she looked away from the sea towards the road. Perhaps it was time she began to think of getting back—she didn't know the city all that well, and she had no idea when the last bus left. Her attention was caught by a tall man walking towards her. The light was in her eyes, so she couldn't see his face clearly, but there was something about him that seemed very familiar. He had almost reached her when realisation dawned, and she sprang to her feet to

watch Dhruv Malhotra cross the last few metres of sand
that separated them and come to stand in front of her.

Her first reaction was of extreme embarrassment.
She'd said a lot more than she'd intended to on the
phone, assuming she'd never see Dhruv again, and she'd
regretted most of it as soon as it was out of her mouth.
She stood speechless, a warm tide of colour staining
her face a dark pink, as Dhruv gently took one of her
hands in his and raised it to his lips.

'I'm sorry,' he said softly. 'I'm sorry I suggested
you'd marry me for the money. I'm sorry I didn't try
harder. And most of all I'm sorry I said I don't love you.'

Riya kept staring at him, hardly believing what she
was hearing.

'I couldn't stop thinking about you,' he said softly.
'I tried to tell myself it was just sex. I tried to push you
out of my mind. But I couldn't. I went all the way back
to college and I wandered around the campus for hours,
trying to recapture what we had then. I was a fool to
throw it away. We could have had so much more time together. You're the world to me, Riya. You complete me.
I realised it when you left that day, but I'd been denying
it for so long it took me a while to come to my senses.'

Riya looked at him suspiciously as she found her
voice. 'You said you were a good liar,' she reminded
him. 'How do I know you're not fibbing to get me back
into your bed? You didn't even tell me you were in Hong
Kong,' she added, her sense of injury getting the better
of her. 'You let me think you were in India, and I said
all those things without knowing that you were lurking
around five feet away.'

'Look at me,' he said, and then, as she stared muti-
nously towards the sea, 'No, *look* at me, Riya.' He took
her chin between his thumb and forefinger and carefully

angled her face up so that she was looking directly into his eyes. 'I love you,' he said, slowly and deliberately.

She saw the sincerity in his golden eyes, and the love, and a little bit of self-doubt. That tinge of vulnerability was what convinced her, and she melted suddenly, like an ice-cream left out too long in the sun.

'I love you, too, Dhruv,' she said, flinging her arms around his neck and hugging him so tightly that he could hardly breathe. 'So much.' And then, realising that she was almost strangling him, she loosened her hold and leaned back a little, smiling into his eyes. 'So you believe in love now?' she asked, almost accusingly. 'And romance?'

'I'm a complete convert,' he said, bending down to kiss her slowly and tenderly, as if she was the most precious thing in the world. 'It took me a long time to get my head around it. I was so sure that I wasn't capable of love. But when I finally accepted that the reason I couldn't do without you was because I loved you it seemed so obvious I almost caught a plane immediately to come after you. Then I remembered how badly I'd upset you by talking about money. So I thought I'd first try and sort out your parents' house as a kind of apology.'

'I almost died of shock when my mum said you'd been home,' Riya said reproachfully. 'I couldn't imagine what you were up to. Some warning would have been nice.'

She leaned her head against his chest for a moment, and then looked up straight into his eyes.

'Are you sure you love me, Dhruv?' she asked quietly. 'I don't think I could bear it if you realised later that you'd made a mistake.'

'I've never been so sure of anything in my life,'

Dhruv said, his heart twisting a little at the lingering uncertainty in her eyes. He released her and pushed her back gently a couple of steps when she continued to cling to him. 'I want to do this properly,' he said and, taking a little box out of his pocket, he dropped to one knee in front of Riya.

'Riya Kumar, I'm completely and irrevocably in love with you. I can't live without you, and I might go completely insane if I have to stay away from you any longer. I promise to love you and cherish you, and to be your devoted slave for the rest of your life. Will you do me the honour of becoming my wife?' he asked.

Riya laughed, though there were tears in her eyes as well. 'Yes,' she said in a whisper, and he slid the platinum eternity band onto her finger and jumped up to pull her into his arms and kiss her thoroughly.

She emerged from his embrace with a flushed face and tousled hair. 'People are looking at us,' she whispered, hiding her face in his chest.

'They can go to hell,' he said firmly, and pulled her into his arms to kiss her again, whispering into her ear, 'Can you try to bother just a *little* bit less about what other people think?'

The wedding was three months later in Mumbai, all Dhruv's suggestions of having a small, low-key family affair having been completely overruled by Riya's mother *and* his. The rituals were a hotchpotch of the customs in the bride's family and in the groom's, and no one except the *pundit* was completely clear about what exactly was happening. Relatives milled around happily all over the place, and even Aunty Seema looked pleased. Gaurav and his mother, of course, were ecstatic.

'Put her down,' Dhruv said exasperatedly as Gaurav and a bunch of Riya's male cousins hoisted her onto their shoulders before the *var-mala* ceremony.

The idea was to make it difficult for the groom to get at her and put the wedding garland round her neck—Gaurav, in spite of being Dhruv's cousin, had shamelessly aligned himself with the bride's relatives in all the traditional games that were played before the wedding. The groom wasn't playing along, though, staying put and refusing to allow his own relatives to lift him up.

'Put her down,' he said again firmly and, leaning forward, whispered something into the boys' ears.

Riya found herself back on *terra firma,* much to her relief, and her future husband smiled down at her as he slipped the garland around her neck.

'Did you bribe them?' she asked suspiciously, as the grinning boys backed off a few paces.

'Of course he did,' Gaurav said scornfully. 'Your husband's a devious man. But you're lucky he did. That sari seems very precariously tied, if you ask me. The whole thing would have fallen off the way they were pulling you around.'

Riya laughed and went to take her place beside Dhruv. He managed to look cool and urbane in spite of all the chaos surrounding him—he'd refused to wear traditional Indian clothes on the grounds that he felt ridiculous in them, and was dressed in one of his usual impeccably cut suits.

'You look more like James Bond than a bridegroom,' she muttered into his ear as she sat down next to him.

'You, on the other hand, look gorgeous,' he whispered back.

He'd never seen her look so lovely. Her large, kohl-rimmed eyes were glowing, and her face was ethereally beautiful under the red *ghunghat*. She'd decided to dispense with the heavy gold jewellery normally worn by the bride, and was instead wearing only a necklace and bangle set that had belonged to her mother, and to her grandmother before that. The heavy red, green and gold wedding sari was draped in almost perfect folds around her slim body, and she looked like a goddess—a very young and mischievous one, but a goddess all the same.

'*Itna mat dekho, nazaar lag jayegi*. Don't stare at her like that, you'll draw the Evil Eye onto her.' An elderly aunt clucked as she reached out to put a *kaala tikka* on Riya's cheek to draw away the evil one.

Dhruv looked away—he wasn't superstitious in the least, but he didn't want the slightest thing to mar their perfect day.

Three hours later, after the *pheras* were done and the guests had mostly headed towards the buffet dinner, Dhruv leaned over to whisper into Riya's ear, 'You want to get out of here?'

Riya turned, startled. 'We can't, can we?' she whispered back. 'We're the star performers in the show. We can't vanish halfway through! Besides, I'm not even sure if we're legally married yet.'

'Don't kid yourself,' Dhruv said drily. 'Right now the star attraction is the chicken biryani. The magistrate's already registered the wedding, you have your *mangalsutra* aro und your neck and we're done with the *pheras*. We're as legal as can be. Come on.' He stood up and held a hand out to her, and as she hesitated added mock-threateningly, 'Riya, if you want my co-operation in giving you those three fat little babies you want, you'll need to start listening to me once in a while.'

She laughed and stood up, giving the *pundit* a half-apologetic look as they left. He raised a cheerful hand in benediction and Dhruv swung her up, striding out of the *mandap,* carrying his bride in his arms. Riya buried her face in his shoulder as a few of the younger men who were still hanging around whistled and clapped. He finally set her back on her feet in the parking lot, and for a few seconds she gazed into his eyes, the mingled passion and tenderness in them blotting out the all the confusion and heartache of the past.

The spell was broken at the sound of approaching voices, and Dhruv held the car door for her before striding around to slide into the driver's seat.

He started the engine so that the air-conditioning came on, but didn't shift the car into gear, turning instead to get something out of the back seat. Riya's eyes widened as he uncorked a bottle of champagne and poured the wine into two glasses.

'Here's to the rest of our lives together,' he said, clinking his glass gently against hers.

'You'll get booked for drunken driving and spend your wedding night in jail,' she said critically, after he'd had a sip.

He laughed and handed his glass to her. 'I have very...*detailed* plans on how I want to spend our wedding night,' he said, his eyes promising all kinds of wicked delights. 'The champagne can wait.'

He reversed the car out of the parking lot, and within a few minutes they were speeding down Marine Drive.

Riya rolled the window down, letting the cool sea breeze wreak havoc on her elaborate coiffure. 'Today's the happiest day of my life,' she said suddenly, and Dhruv's heart turned over at the simple avowal.

'Mine, too,' he replied, more moved than he had ever been before.

He burst into a laughter a second later, though, as she turned limpid eyes towards him and said, 'I'm hoping the night will be even better.'

And it was.

* * * * *